THE *NEXT ONE WILL KILL YOU*

AN ANGUS GREEN NOVEL

NEIL S. PLAKCY

DIVERSIONBOOKS

Diversion Books
A Division of Diversion Publishing Corp.
443 Park Avenue South, Suite 1008
New York, New York 10016
www.DiversionBooks.com

For more information, email info@diversionbooks.com

First Diversion Books edition November 2016.
Print ISBN: 978-1-68230-301-6
eBook ISBN: 978-1-68230-300-9

To my parents,
who introduced me to the love of reading
in general, and crime fiction in particular.

1
UNEXPECTED AUDIENCE

I was determined to help my brother, even if I had to strip naked in front of a crowd of rowdy drunks to do it. Which was why I had laid out a range of clothes on my bed, from my baggiest sweatpants and a XXL T-shirt an old boyfriend had left behind, down to a pair of boxers and a jockstrap.

"What's the matter, Angus? Can't make up your mind what to wear?" my roommate Jonas asked as he stuck his head into my bedroom.

"No, I'm wearing all of it," I said. "I signed up for the gay strip trivia contest at Lazy Dick's tonight. My little brother has a chance to go on a study abroad program to Italy next summer, and I want to win the thousand-dollar prize for him."

"You're crazy," Jonas said.

"I've been boning up on gay trivia ever since I found out about the contest," I said.

"Boning up," Jonas said, giggling.

"Go on, get out of here," I said. "I've got to get dressed."

When I finished I looked in the mirror. I have a skinny frame, and the bulk the layers of clothes gave me was flattering. I've been told I have a friendly, open face. It gets me a lot of attention at gay bars. Or maybe my pecs, which I work on religiously, are the key. Either way, I usually drink for free.

I drove over to the club in my brand-new Mini Cooper. I had never owned a car before, scrambling around Penn State on foot, by bus, or hitching rides with friends, and I still couldn't believe it was mine. My friends had told me to buy the convertible model, but with my fair skin I would have been a walking sunburn.

Lazy Dick's is a sprawling bar right in the heart of Wilton Manors, a suburb of Fort Lauderdale. A covered patio with large tables surrounding a dance floor wraps around the front of the single-story building. The younger guys—and the older men chasing them—hang out on the patio, under a grass roof festooned with Mardi Gras beads, beer ads, and pinups of whoever is appearing at the local strip clubs. When I pulled into the parking lot I could hear Cher blasting from the speakers and smell the beer and testosterone.

I walked inside, where it's darker and more intimate, with cozy booths for two. The lighting is dim and flatters those who haven't had work done yet. I found the emcee, a plus-sized drag queen named Helen Wheels, and signed in with her.

I waited nervously for the call to the stage, sweating under all those layers of clothing. Then I heard someone say, "Finally, a familiar face in this joint."

I turned around to see Vito Mastroianni, a fellow special agent from the FBI field office in Miami. He was with Roly Gutierrez, another agent, and I was stunned to see them there. As far as I knew, both guys were straight, which meant this wasn't a recreational visit. Roly worked on the Joint Terrorism Task Force, while Vito and I were assigned to the Violent Crimes Task Force, though not to the same cases. Was there some kind of international or domestic terrorism going on at Lazy Dick's? Was I right in the middle of the action?

I remembered a clause in some paperwork I'd filled out when I first joined the FBI. Something about sexual behavior of a public nature which reflected a lack of discretion or judgment. If I lost, could I get away without shucking my jockstrap?

They couldn't be there to warn me from entering the contest. How could they have known I'd be in it anyway? It wasn't like my redheaded mug had been in any of the ads. And I was sure they both had better things to do on a Sunday night than make sure I didn't wag my weenie in public.

So what the hell were Roly and Vito doing at Lazy Dick's?

"Need your help, rookie," Vito said. "We were supposed to meet a source here and he hasn't shown up, and nobody's willing to tell us squat about him."

"A source? What kind of source?"

"Angus Green!"

I looked over, and Helen Wheels was waving in my direction. "We're ready to go on."

"I have to... I'm supposed to..." I stuttered.

"Go on, we'll wait," Roly said. I watched them return to a table in the front row as I got in line behind Helen.

The other contestants and I trooped up behind her like ducklings following Mama. The Sondheim tune playing in the background stopped abruptly and the spotlight came on—but a few feet to the left of Helen. "Hello! Over here!" she called, and the light moved to her.

She introduced each of us, to accompanying applause and catcalls. There were ten of us in the competition, from a couple of older men to the guy on my right, a bodybuilder with glazed eyes who was probably just there to show off his amazing buffness.

I was right; he flubbed the first question, about which gay icon's death in 1969 was alleged to have played a part in the Stonewall Riots. "The rainbow flag?" he asked.

Well, that was a gay icon, all right, but rumors of its death have been greatly exaggerated.

The audience buzzed him with raspberries. "No, I'm sorry, that's not correct," Helen said. "It's time to lose an article of clothing."

The guy shrugged and pulled off his T-shirt, and the crowd cheered to see his washboard abs and bulging pecs. He performed a couple of bodybuilder poses, and someone in the audience called, "Work it, baby!"

Helen primped her black bouffant hairdo and passed the question to me. I answered, "Judy Garland."

At the end of the first round, I was still fully clothed and sweating under the hot lights. Helen said, "Let's have a round of tequila for our contestants," and Kyle, the blond twink bartender, walked down the row handing us shots.

I wasn't about to flub my chance to win by getting drunk. Fortunately I had begun to tend bar once I legally could, and I'd learned how to take a shot without drinking it.

I waited until everyone had shots in hand, and we all leaned our heads back at the same time. I covered my shot glass with both hands and tossed the glass back—just to the right of my mouth, so that the tequila went flying behind me instead of inside me.

The crowd was too busy cheering to notice my trick. Unfortunately, the questions got harder as the rounds progressed, and within half an hour I'd kicked off both shoes and both socks, pulled off my oversized T-shirt, and even dropped my baggy sweats.

It was hard to focus on the game knowing that Roly and Vito were in the audience. I'd been out and proud since my first days at the Bureau but there was something different about looking like a fool in front of two FBI veterans. What would they think of me? What would they say about me at the office? And what kind of source could Vito and Roly possibly be meeting at a gay bar in Wilton Manors?

Once there were fewer of us on stage, I couldn't pretend to drink the tequila shots anymore and I had to begin downing them. After more rounds passed, I was left on stage with a brainiac named Andrew. He was a trivia machine, and there was no way I was going to beat him. I could see the prize money fluttering away from me. Second place was only a hundred bucks, which would only buy my brother a couple of pizzas in Italy.

I thought about quitting, before I embarrassed myself any further. Stumble off the stage, find Vito and Roly, and jump back into the role of newly-minted FBI special agent, one I had worked hard to achieve.

We went through another couple of rounds, and Andrew began to falter. I could still win. But could I hold onto my job, too? I really wanted to be able to give that thousand bucks to Danny. Give my little bro the opportunity to roam the hills of Tuscany, absorb the culture and flirt with the *belle ragazze*.

"Angus?" Helen asked.

I looked over at her. Andrew had flubbed a question while I was freaking out. His hand was in the waistband of his briefs, ready to drop them and cede the cash to me if I could get the question right.

"You have an answer?" Helen asked.

"Can you repeat the question?"

Helen sighed theatrically, and her fake boobs threatened to jump out of her dress and assault Vito and Roly in the front row. "What lesbian or feminist symbol was first used in the Nazi concentration camps? If you get this right, Angus, you're our winner. Get it wrong, and you go into sudden death with Andrew."

My first thought was the pink triangle. But was that just for gay men? I closed my eyes and concentrated. And then I remembered a lesbian I had known through the Rainbow Roundtable at Penn State. She'd had a black triangle appliquéd to her backpack, and I'd asked her about the significance of it.

I opened my eyes and smiled. Looking right at my FBI colleagues, I said, "The black triangle."

The audience was quiet, until Helen said, "That is correct. You are our winner!"

Kyle handed Helen a lavender sash and a paper crown, and she kissed me on both cheeks, then draped the sash around my neck. It was cheap polyester and made my bare chest itch, but I didn't care. She put the crown on my head, and I blew kisses to the crowd. I was so excited—I'd won the money for Danny.

When I finished bowing and pirouetting, the house lights came up. The glare was startling, and as my bar buddies came up to congratulate me, I struggled to get my eyes to focus. After all the kissing and hugging was done, I pulled on my shorts and T-shirt, and carried the rest of my crap over to the table where Roly and Vito sat, empty beer glasses in front of them.

It was funny to see them out of their normal FBI drag—dark suits, white shirts, power ties. Vito wore an XXL New York Jets T-shirt, while Roly, a lot slimmer, advertised his allegiance to the Miami Dolphins. Straight guys in a gay bar. Of course they'd wear football shirts, as if they were proclaiming their heterosexuality. Didn't they know that some gay guys were sports buffs? With that curl of black chest hair coming out of the top of his shirt, big, beefy Vito screamed "bear," and I could see a couple of guys eyeing him.

I took the third seat. "Roly. Vito. You have anything else to tell me before I start talking to people?"

"Not while you're drunk," Roly replied. "Monday morning, we're going to have a meeting. The three of us. Then you can get started."

They both stood up. Vito said, "Yo, rookie, there's no rule that you have to carry your weapon with you when you're off duty, but most of us do. Doesn't look like you are, unless you've got a Glock 22 in your shorts. " He snickered.

They walked toward the door. I looked after them, and I could see those twenty weeks of training at the FBI academy in Quantico go out the window, along with my job in the Miami field office and my dream of doing something more exciting with my life than preparing tax returns. I ran for the bathroom, reaching the toilet just as I let go all that tequila.

2
CRIMINAL ACTIVITY

I couldn't drive home, so I hitched a ride with Jonas, and I had him stop at the bank so I could deposit the cash I'd won. After I took a long hot shower, I transferred the money from my account to Danny's. Then I went back over what Roly and Vito could have been doing at Lazy Dick's. What kind of information could their source have been able to provide?

I'd spent years working in bars and restaurants and knew all kinds of criminal activity that could go on in one. Managers who skimmed the register to pay off gambling debts, bartenders who served up everything from marijuana to steroids along with drafts and cocktails, and a sous chef who had walked off with whole slabs of beef and bottles of pricey champagne, which he sold to the restaurant down the street.

Was any of that important enough to merit FBI interest? There were always rumors that bars, particularly gay bars, had ties to organized crime. Hell, that had been news back in the days of Stonewall. But was it the case in Wilton Manors?

More importantly, how would Roly and Vito handle seeing me at Lazy Dick's, participating in the strip trivia contest? I'd never lied to the FBI about being gay. Any cursory investigation would have turned up my role of treasurer to the Rainbow Roundtable at Penn State, and a host of other activities I'd participated in.

I knew both Roly and Vito, but just to say "hello" to. There was no reason why they'd be picked to spy on me. And it wasn't like I was delivering strip-o-grams dressed in FBI gear or anything. I hadn't violated any laws. Hell, I hadn't even shown my three-piece set up there.

Though most of my time was spent behind a desk, I loved it when I had the chance to go out in the field. There were bad guys out there, and I was doing my part to stop them. I was doing a good job, and every day I was learning something new. Had I thrown it all away in a few moments of near-nudity?

Late that night, my phone beeped with an e-mail from Danny, thanking me for the cash. At the end he wrote, "Gotta talk to you soon, bro. Things going on up here."

Things? What kind of things? School things? Girlfriend things? Danny was as resolutely hetero as I was homo, and movie-actor handsome. Since puberty he'd been surrounded by a coterie of adoring females. He was smart, too, and though he had a part-time job at the same restaurant where I'd worked, I made sure he stayed focused on school.

Our father had died when I was ten and Danny was five, and our mother remarried about five years later. Our mom's second husband was an okay guy, but he refused to give either of us a penny to go to college. I'd worked my way through a bachelor's and a master's in five years at Penn State as a waiter and bartender, accumulating a boatload of student loans because I had to cover what the school thought Mom and Roger should. I wanted to make things easier for Danny.

Danny looked up to me, and I'd always taken care of him. After our dad died, I let him cry, let him sleep in my bed, walked him to and from school every day holding his hand. When I hit puberty and realized I was attracted to guys, not girls, I freaked out, worried I might infect Danny or something, but when he was ten I caught him making out with the little girl next door, and I relaxed.

I looked at the clock; it was 1 a.m. Should I call him? Or wait for him to call me? I'd wait. It might turn out to be nothing, or work itself out.

When my alarm went off at 7 a.m. I didn't feel like I'd slept at all. I was at my desk reviewing weekend surveillance reports when Roly came to my office door. "Conference room," he said. "Now."

Roly was a Cuban-American guy who'd been in the Miami office for a dozen years, turning down promotions to stay near his family. He was a snazzy dresser, always wearing tailored suits. He'd brought a machine into the office to make Cuban coffee and he often brought tiny cups of it he called *cortaditos* to meetings.

I followed him down the hall, figuring that he and Vito would fill me in on their investigation. Vito was Italian-American, a career FBI guy who had moved around the country, getting a promotion each time. Like every male agent, he wore a dark suit to work, though he often switched the standard white shirt for a pale blue or green one. He was heftier and taller than Roly, but they were both the kind of guys whose looks screamed "federal agent."

I hadn't mastered the FBI look yet. I bought my suits at a warehouse store and my white shirts at Sawgrass Mills, the big outlet mall. When I looked in the mirror after getting dressed, sometimes I felt like a little kid wearing an adult costume.

My adrenaline level soared when we reached the conference room and I saw the Special Agent in Charge in the conference room talking to Vito. Had the SAC vetoed my chance to help Vito and Roly when he discovered I'd taken my clothes off in order to win a measly thousand bucks?

I hesitated in the doorway as Roly slid into a chair next to the SAC, a middle-aged guy, neatly trimmed hair, ordinary suit. "Come in, Agent Green. Sit down," the SAC said, motioning to a chair next to Vito. He looked like any attorney or accountant you'd run into on the commuter trains in the northeast. "You're working on the armored car detail, aren't you?"

"Yes, sir," I said as I sat.

"I've heard you're doing good work there. They're going to be sorry to lose you."

My mouth dropped open. "You can't fire me for taking my clothes off. I wasn't even naked."

The SAC's eyebrows rose. "Nobody's firing you," he said. "Though you should be careful where you've been taking your clothes off. Roly and Vito have asked to have you transferred to a case they're working. Any problems with that?"

I shook my head, my stomach churning and my head spinning. "No, sir."

"Good." He stood up. "Young agents need good mentors. You've got two of the best here. I expect you to learn from them."

"Yes sir." I waited until he had left the room to turn to Roly and Vito and say, "Now will one of you please tell me what the fuck is going on?"

3
UNIQUE TALENTS

"What's going on is that you got yourself right in the middle of a tip that came in," Vito said, leaning back in his chair so far that I worried the buttons on his white shirt might burst over his stomach.

"An interesting one that has come to a dead end," Roly said. "We're hoping you can use your unique talents to give us a jump start."

I slumped back in my chair. "I thought I was getting fired."

"Yeah, that was kind of fun to watch," Vito said.

I glared at him. "You're going to mentor me—you might try being nicer."

"Niceness is not Vito's specialty," Roly said. "So, call came into the tip line and it got routed to me. Take a look at the report."

He slid a manila folder across the table to me. I opened it and saw a single sheet of paper inside, the contact form we filled out each time we spoke with an informant or did any investigation. "Paco?" I asked. "All you got was Paco? Isn't that a common Spanish nickname?"

"Read the material, rookie," Vito said.

Paco, whoever he was, had called our tip line from a number that couldn't be traced and said that he had information on a possible breach of homeland security.

Well, he hadn't said it in those words, but the operator had figured that out and routed his call to Roly as a member of the Joint Terrorism Task Force, one of nine FBI squads under the broad umbrella of counter-terrorism. The JTTF included thirty-eight participating agencies with over a hundred and fifty personnel, many of them from local law enforcement agencies detailed to work with us full-time on domestic terrorism.

Roly had taken careful notes on his conversation with Paco, who had worked for a food vendor at the Miami Beach Convention Center and knew all the back entrances and where security was stationed. He gave specific examples. "These true?" I asked, looking up.

"Would we have been waiting around at a gay bar if it wasn't?" Vito asked.

I was still pissed about the way I'd been tricked. "I don't know anything about your personal life."

Vito scowled. "Watch it."

"Boys. Play nice," Roly warned, but there was a hint of a smile on his face.

I was being invited into a case that might be a lot more interesting than sitting behind my computer analyzing data. Time to stop acting like a child and be professional.

I continued to read. Someone had paid Paco a thousand bucks to draw a diagram of the convention center and identify all the security breaches he knew about. He didn't know what was being planned, but he was worried they were going to do something to hurt people. That was why he had come to the FBI.

Roly had asked him a series of questions, and the end result was that it didn't look like terrorism, but a plan to rob some of the jewelry wholesalers at an upcoming trade show at the convention center.

"This trade show," I said. "The wholesalers coming from outside the state?"

"All around the country as well as a few international dealers," Roly said.

That was why Vito was involved; he worked in the Violent Crimes Unit, which handled a whole range of criminal activities, from those on the high seas—cruise ships and container ships—to theft of art, jewelry, or other high-priced items. Pretty much anything that was a violation of the Hobbes Act, which governed interstate commerce. So any theft that occurred there could technically be considered a Hobbes Act case, giving the FBI jurisdiction.

"The show kicks off in mid-October, a week from this Thursday," Roly said. "It's one of the biggest in the country, and attracts buyers and sellers from around the world. Over a hundred million dollars in precious gems will be there."

He shot back the cuffs on his immaculately tailored black suit and rested his forearms on the conference room table. "We had a tip that there's a major theft in the works. Source was supposed to meet us last night at that bar but he never showed."

I was curious about the choice of a gay bar for a

rendezvous. "Did Paco pick Lazy Dick's, or did you?" I asked.

"He did," Roly said. "He said he was a busboy there, and that he'd slip us the information when he was clearing our table. But after a while with no contact, we asked our waiter if Paco was there. He said Paco hadn't showed up for work."

"Running into you was our only piece of luck," Vito said. "We didn't know it was a gay bar or we would have sent you in the first place."

So they knew I was gay, even when they hardly knew me. "Seriously?" I asked. "A bar in Wilton Manors. Called Lazy Dick's. You guys had no clue the clientele would be gay? Doesn't say much for your intelligence-gathering abilities."

"I live in Miami," Roly said, as if that explained it. "You tell me a bar on South Beach; sure, I wonder if it's one of the gay ones. Vito here is the Fort Lauderdale expert."

"I know there are gay guys in Wilton Manors," Vito said defensively. "But I didn't realize the bars were so, you know, segregated. We have a gay couple that lives across the street from us in Cooper City. They go to the same restaurants and stores we do."

"Be that as it may," Roly said. "You saw the way Vito and I stood out in that bar. Nobody was going to talk to us. You, though, they'll talk to. Find Paco, and find out what he knows. Then come back and tell us, and we'll figure out how to proceed."

"You want me to go in there and start asking about a jewelry heist?"

"No, rookie," Vito said, adjusting the shoulders of his plus-sized suit. "We want you to go in there and be your charming self. Chat guys up. See if Paco comes back to work, and if not, find out who he hung around with, what he might have known. And remember, intelligence is like milk. It goes sour after a couple of days."

"When you find anything, run it past me or Vito," Roly said. "We'll be around, but this case is yours from now on."

"You're not working it with me?"

"You pull us in when you need resources."

I nearly tripped over my feet in my eagerness to get back to my desk. The first thing I did was a search on the trade show. But I couldn't find much online except the contact information for the show's organizers. I called the number from the website, introduced myself, and asked to speak to whoever was in charge of security.

A guy came on the line and introduced himself as the event manager. "We contract out for our security," he said. "Why is the FBI interested? Have you heard something?"

"I'm just doing background. That's why I want to talk to your security guy."

"The company's called SecurEvent, and our contact is Navillus Sullivan."

I wrote the information down, then looked at it. "You realize his first name is just his last name spelled backwards."

"Doesn't bother me," the guy said.

I called SecurEvent and spoke to Sullivan. I figured he already knew the backwards spelling thing so I didn't mention it to him. He told me that if I drove up to his office in Hollywood he could show me all the information he had.

It was a gorgeous day, sunlight glinting off the retention ponds around our headquarters—which also served as a deterrent for a vehicular attack on the buildings. I rolled down my windows and got onto the highway with a light heart. I hadn't been fired, and I'd been given my own case. Now all I had to do was not fuck it up.

I found SecurEvent's office in a modern complex on Hollywood Boulevard a couple of blocks off I-95, surrounded by the kind of tall palm trees that were everywhere in South Florida. Sullivan was a tall, rangy Jamaican in his mid-forties, with coffee-colored skin and a buzz cut. His mellow accent was a contrast to his brusque demeanor.

We sat down in his office, and he passed a sheet of paper toward me. "This is a list of all the registered vendors," he said.

I looked at it. "Any idea who would be most vulnerable? Who's bringing the most money, or the most gemstones?"

"No way to know that. These guys are very close-mouthed."

"Tell me what you have planned in the way of security."

He handed me a glossy brochure. "We begin by meeting with the client to assess any possible security risks. We consult with our clients to create a staffing and deployment plan that is tailored to meet the venue's specific features."

"I can read that in the brochure," I said. "Talk to me about this particular show."

"This is our first year handling security for this show. So I spent a lot of time walking around the convention center, evaluating ways in and out—where the dealers will park, what hours people will be around before and after the show, and so on." He handed me a map of the building. "You'll see everything marked here. A lot of the dealers bring their own security, so we had to establish a credentialing procedure. And I'll have undercover agents on the show floor as well as uniformed operatives at each entrance."

He handed me another sheet. "These are the personnel we'll have on hand. I have personally reviewed every single one, checking references. We'll also have a fully stocked facility with a nurse practitioner on duty in case of medical emergency."

He walked me through the procedures he had in place for the show's setup and takedown, as well as the days when it was open to the public. After two hours, my eyes were crossed and I couldn't see any flaws in his plans.

He walked me out to the front door. "If you come up with any information about threats, you'll share it with us, won't you?" he asked. "We have a good working relationship with the Miami Beach Police Department."

"Most likely we'll work directly with MBPD, and then they can choose what to share with you," I said. "Remember, we don't have any concrete information about a threat to the show or anyone who's attending. This is just background."

He frowned. "You've got the Bureau line down well."

"Thank you for your cooperation. I'll be in touch."

As I walked out to the parking lot, I saw the sign for one of the big discount stores across the street, and remembered that Helen Wheels worked in the garden center there. Time to turn on the charm. I would show Vito and Roly that I could get the inside information they couldn't.

4
AGENT CUTIE PIE

I found Helen Wheels spraying trays of purple and white pansies. He looked a lot different in his red apron, his head shaved, with a pair of reading glasses on a chain around his neck. "Hey, cutie pie," he said. "What brings you up here? Want to buy a nice cactus?" He pointed at a display of appropriately phallic succulents.

"No thanks. I'm here on business. Can we talk somewhere?"

"Sure. I've got a break coming." We walked through the store to the small café, where I bought him a cup of coffee. "So, what business are you in, cutie pie?" he asked.

"It's Agent Cutie Pie," I said, showing him my badge.

He fanned himself. "Oh, my. So adorable, and a special agent too. I am 100 percent at your service."

"You know a busboy at Lazy Dick's named Paco?" I asked.

He looked at me closely. "This some kind of immigration thing?"

I shook my head. "That's a whole different agency."

"Because I wouldn't want to get anybody in trouble." Helen sat back. "But Paco's probably screwed already. He didn't show up for work on Saturday."

"Tell me about him." I pulled out a leather portfolio with a lined pad inside and uncapped my pen.

"Don't know his last name," Helen said. "And Paco? That's probably not his real name anyway."

"Tell me something you do know."

"There's a whole crew of Latinos behind the scenes at Lazy Dick's. The owners, they don't look too closely at papers, if you're willing to work. Paco was one of the busboys, there maybe six months or so. Nice guy, chatty, but straight as a board. Had a wife and kids back in Mexico somewhere."

"What did he chat about?"

Helen shrugged. "Don't know. It was mostly in Spanish."

"You know where he lives?"

"With a bunch of the other busboys and waiters in a house somewhere in Wilted Flowers. Don't know the exact address, but they'd have it in the office."

Wilted Flowers was the local nickname for Wilton Manors, because the area attracted a lot of older gay men— many who had been handsome once, but whose looks had faded with age. "Remember anyone he was particularly friendly with? Somebody I could talk to?"

"What's your interest in Paco, anyway? If this isn't about immigration."

"I can't say. But he's not in trouble, at least not from us. We just want to talk to him."

"Yeah, that's what they all say." Helen stood up. "I've got to get back to work. Thanks for the coffee."

I felt weird when he left, like I'd come out of the closet yet again. I hadn't told anyone at Lazy Dick's that I worked for the FBI. Knowing what a big mouth Helen had, the news was going to be all over the bar before the bell rang to signal the end of happy hour.

That meant that if I expected to get any information, I had to get up there before Helen did. I looked at my watch; it was closing in on three o'clock. I got onto I-95 heading north, dodged through traffic, and was just pulling into the large parking lot when my cell phone rang, Elton John singing "Daniel, my brother."

"This isn't a good time, Danny. I'm working."

"I'm in trouble, Angus. I really need your help."

"What's the matter?" I parked in a spot near the front door.

"The police came to the restaurant yesterday just before the dinner rush. They think one of us is stealing credit card numbers from customers."

Danny had started at Penn State a few months after I graduated, and I'd gotten him a job at the same restaurant where I'd worked, an Italian place called La Scuola, Italian for "The School." It wasn't high cuisine, mostly pizza, calzones, and sub sandwiches with cute names connected to the University—the Nittany 'Zone was a round of salted dough stuffed with mozzarella and ham, folded over into a half-moon and baked in the pizza oven. The Joe Paterno, named for the legendary football coach, was filled with tiny meatballs, and guys used to ask for Joe's Balls—until that whole pedophile scandal knocked him from his pedestal.

"You didn't get arrested, did you?" I asked.

"No. They asked us all a bunch of questions and threatened us—said if we were holding out we'd be in big trouble. I didn't do anything, Angus, I swear."

"You know who might be responsible?" I asked.

His voice wavered. "I don't have a clue. Angus, what if they think it's me? I don't want to go to prison."

"You're not going to prison if you're innocent," I said.

A big black Lincoln eased into the parking lot. A butch older guy with an unlit cigar in his mouth got out, then checked himself out in the side mirror. "Listen, I've got to get into this place and ask some questions while I can," I said. "Here's what I want you to do. Write down everything the cops said to you, as much as you can remember, and e-mail it to me. I'll call you later and we'll talk about it, all right? There are a lot of possibilities."

"I'm freaking out here, Angus. You can't leave me hanging."

"I know, Danny. I'll call you back. I promise."

I ended the call and followed the cigar guy inside, past a display of shirts and other merchandise spangled with puns and sexual innuendos. He turned left, toward the restrooms, and I went into the bar.

Jimmy Buffett was singing on the stereo system about his lost shaker of salt, and two white-haired men down at one end of the outdoor bar looked like they knew just what he was talking about.

The bartender was a rail-thin Trinidadian named Raj with cocoa-colored skin, a smooth island accent, and the habitual runny nose of a coke addict. He was in his early twenties, and wore a skin-tight tank top with the Lazy Dick logo—a penis in a lounge chair, with a straw hat over its head and a pair of hibiscus-patterned board shorts over its balls. "Hey, Raj, what's going on," I said, sliding onto a bar stool.

"Green Hornet," he said. "Don't often see you here so early in the day."

Raj had a nickname for everyone, a riff on the person's real name or appearance. When he'd learned my last name was Green, he'd come up with that reference to the super hero. At least he didn't call me Angus Cattle.

I ordered a virgin strawberry margarita and asked, "You know a busboy here named Paco?"

"Straight," he said. "Wife back in Matamoros."

"Yeah, I don't want to fuck him, I just want to talk to him. He around?"

Raj turned to the fruity drink dispenser behind him and filled a plastic cup. "Whip?" he asked.

"Do me," I said, and he swirled whipped cream on top of my drink, topping it with a maraschino cherry.

Britney Spears was singing in the background now, asking someone to hit her one more time. When Raj handed the drink to me, I said, "So, Paco?"

"What you want to talk to him about?"

It was time to come out. I pulled out my badge. "I work for the FBI, Raj. I need to talk to Paco."

"You're out of luck. He hasn't been to work in a couple of days."

I had a sinking feeling it was Paco who was out of luck. But I said, "I heard he lives with a couple of guys from the bar. You know who?"

Raj hesitated. To my right, shards of afternoon light crept in between the window blinds and I could see dust motes flickering in the air. The bar was quiet except for the low music and the clatter of one of the busboys clearing a table.

"I'm not the ICE-man," I said to Raj. "Not looking to send anybody back home. I just need to find Paco and talk to him."

He leaned in close. "You didn't hear it from me. But talk to Usnavy." He nodded his head toward the noisy busboy, a stocky guy in his mid-twenties with an unruly mop of black curls. The guy hoisted a plastic bin full of dirty dishes and headed toward the kitchen.

Soon after moving to Miami I'd discovered that Usnavy—pronounced "us-navvy"—was a common name for both men and women from Puerto Rico, where the US Navy ships were so prominently docked.

The two older men at the other end of the bar signaled for another round, and Raj went to pull their beers. I sat there sipping my drink, listening to the laughter of a group out on the patio, until I saw Usnavy come out of the swinging kitchen door carrying his plastic bin, now empty.

He started wiping down a table, and I got up and walked over to him. "My name's Angus," I said to him. "I'm looking for Paco. You know where he is?"

His eyes darted from left to right. "No," he mumbled.

"But you live with him, don't you?"

"I have to work," he said, his accent heavy as the burden of a lousy job in a foreign country. He picked up his washcloth and bin.

I pulled out my ID again. "I'm from the FBI. Not ICE. I'm not trying to deport you or any of your roommates. But I need to find Paco."

He put his stuff down and looked at the table. "He leave Saturday afternoon, say he going to work, but he never show up. I not seen him since."

"Any idea where he went?"

He shook his head. "He don't know nobody. And he got no money to go back to Mexico."

That didn't sound good. "Come on, sit down," I said, sliding into the booth and motioning across from me. "Tell me about him. What's his last name?"

He sighed deeply, but slid into the booth. "He say Gonzalez, but I don't think that true. But he a good guy, Paco. Work hard. Always sending money back to his *familia*."

"How long have you known him?"

"Six months, maybe. He work on Miami Beach for long time, then get fired. We used to have guy here, Ricardo, he live in the apartment with us. He knew Paco, help him get job here, and move him in with us. Then Ricardo talk bad to customers one day and get fired. He move out then, but Paco stay. He talk a lot, but mostly just junk. Nobody else that friendly with him."

"What did he talk about?"

"His wife, his babies. He try to make sure everybody know he straight. But you know something? He suck a few dicks for money, like everybody else." He lowered his voice. "Paco do almost anything for cash."

"Anything else?" I asked.

He shrugged. "Sometimes he talk about place he used to work, convention center in Miami Beach. How he so important there, but then he get fired because he have no papers."

"That must have made him angry."

"Yeah. He always talk about how he gonna get back at the man who fired him."

I looked around the restaurant for inspiration, and saw a wall of photos of customers and staff. "His picture up there anywhere?" I asked.

Usnavy stood up and walked over to the wall, and I followed him. He looked up and down, until he picked out a snapshot of a couple of staff with some of the customers, taken at the Labor Day party a month before. "That him," he said, pointing to a round-faced guy with dark hair and a five o'clock shadow. "And there, that Ricardo."

The man he pointed to, at the other end of the group, was a sallow-faced Hispanic with bad acne scars. And right in the middle of the lineup was my roommate Jonas.

5

A NATURAL REDHEAD

I reached up and unpinned the photo. "Thanks, Usnavy," I said.

"You look out for Paco. He a good guy."

I was about to say, "Only the good die young," but I didn't know for sure that Paco was dead. I just had a bad feeling about his chances of survival.

Usnavy picked up his washcloth and bin and disappeared back into the kitchen. A mixed group of men and women walked in, a couple wearing polo shirts with the crest of Fort Lauderdale High, down the street, and Raj got busy serving them.

I couldn't take Usnavy's and Raj's word for it that Paco wasn't there. I had to check for myself. So I followed Usnavy through the swinging doors.

"Hey, no customers in here," a bald cook in a white apron said.

I held up my badge. "FBI. I'm looking for Paco Gonzalez."

"Not here," the cook said. "Hasn't been here for a couple of days. Didn't even call."

I walked around, looking at each of the five guys in the room. None of them matched the photo of Paco. I ended with the cook. "What's your name?"

"You want to see my papers?"

The kitchen had ground to a halt as everyone stopped to listen to us. I smelled onions, grease, and a stinky aroma I recognized as Brussels sprouts sautéing with bacon.

"No, I just want to know who I'm talking to."

"Eddie. Eduardo Réal. I got my driver's license in my wallet, in my locker."

"Don't need to see it. When was the last time you saw Paco?"

Eddie looked around. "Friday?" he asked.

There was general assent.

"Know anywhere he could have gone?"

Dead silence. I opened my wallet and started passing out cards. "If any of you hear anything, see Paco, whatever, call me."

"There a reward?" Eddie asked.

"Service to your country," I said. "And you never know when you can use a friend in the FBI."

"Like I need that kind of friend," Eddie muttered.

"Maybe you don't," I said mildly. "But somebody else might. I have a feeling Paco could use a friend right now."

Nobody said anything more, so I walked back out through the swinging door. My half-finished virgin daiquiri was still sitting at the booth where I'd spoken with Usnavy, but I'd lost my appetite for it.

I knocked on the door to the office door. The butch older guy I'd walked in behind answered. He looked at me and said, "Auditions for dancers are on Thursday afternoons." Then he tried to close the door.

I held up my badge. "FBI," I said. "Thanks for the tip about the auditions, but I've got some questions about one of your employees."

He peered at the badge. He was wearing a sweatshirt with the sleeves rolled up, and his graying chest hair poked out around his neck. He looked back at me. "You look familiar. You sure you haven't auditioned before?"

I shook my head. "But I won the strip trivia contest Sunday night."

"That's it," he said, stepping back. "Just didn't recognize you with your clothes on. I'm Barry Weiner. General Manager. How can I help you?"

I avoided the obvious joke about a guy named Weiner working at a gay bar. "I'm looking for Paco Gonzalez. What can you tell me about him?"

"He gave me a valid Social Security card. That's all I know."

"I'm not from Immigration," I said, for about the fifth time that day. "You have an address on him?"

He turned to a file cabinet and pulled out a folder. Inside were photocopies of Paco's ID card and Social Security card, along with a job application. I wrote down where he lived, along with the information on his wife in Matamoros. "This his current address?" I asked.

"Far as I know. He lives with a bunch of the guys from

the kitchen." He sat down in a worn wooden chair. "If you're not looking at him for an immigration violation, what's he in trouble for?"

"He made contact with the Bureau himself," I said. "Said he had some information to share. But he didn't show up for the appointment. So I'm looking for him."

"Information about what?"

I wasn't about to tell him, so I said, "I'm just the errand boy. Nobody tells me why I'm doing something, just to do it."

"Yeah, I know what that's like," Weiner said.

I gave him my card. "If he shows up, or you hear anything about him, will you give me a call?"

"Sure thing." I turned to walk out and he said, "Hey, if Uncle Sam isn't paying you well enough, you can always come back for those auditions," he said. "You showed off a good body at strip trivia on Sunday night. You a natural redhead?"

"If I had a quarter for every time a guy asked me that at a gay bar, I wouldn't need to work for Uncle Sam," I said as I walked out.

I sat in my car and called Roly and told him what I'd found so far. "You have a contact at the morgue?" I asked. "I figure that's the next place to look for Paco."

"Yeah, talk to an assistant ME there named Maria Fleitas. She can help you out." He gave me her phone number.

I dialed and asked to speak with Dr. Fleitas, and sat there on hold in the Lazy Dick's parking lot for a while. Palm fronds danced in the light breeze, and a steady stream of traffic cruised down Wilton Drive, everything from beat-up pickup trucks to a bright blue Bentley convertible so new it still had its temporary tag. Eddie Real came out the back door of the kitchen, hopped on a green scooter, and took off, and I wondered where he was going. Was his shift over, or had I spooked him?

When Maria Fleitas came on the line, there was noise in the background, something like a saw. I didn't want to think about what was being cut open. "How can I help you?" she asked.

I identified myself and said that Roly Gutierrez had given me her name. "I'm tracking a missing person. Thought he might be spending some time with you. Hispanic male, thirty, born and raised in Mexico." I looked at the photo. "Dark hair, round face, about five foot six or so. Sound familiar?"

"BSO brought in a floater yesterday that matches that general description," she said. "You have next of kin to do an ID?"

"Not yet. How about if I come over and compare him to a picture I have?"

"Always happy to get an ID on a Juan Doe," she said.

Before heading to the morgue, I detoured past the address Barry Weiner had given me. It was a small apartment building on Andrews Avenue, a few blocks down from the gay and lesbian community center. Two stories, with a rusted railing along the stairs to the second floor. A dying palm tree stood out front, its fronds brown and drooping, coconut husks and dog poop around its base.

I walked up the stairs and knocked on the door of apartment eight.

No answer. I knocked again, but I hadn't expected anyone to be there.

I had turned to go when the next door opened, and

a skeletally thin man with oxygen tubes in his nose stuck his head outside. "Nobody's home there," he said. "They're all at work."

"Thanks." I showed him Paco's photo. "You seen this guy lately?"

He shook his head. "Not since Saturday afternoon. Drove off with a friend of his."

"You know the friend?"

"That one there." He pointed at Ricardo in the picture. "Used to live in the apartment," he said. "Don't know his name. Can't keep all them straight anyway."

He laughed, and the laughed devolved into a cough. I didn't know what to do—pat him on the back, call 911, or wait it out. I settled for the third option. "Sorry," he said, when he finally stopped. "Crack myself up sometimes. Ain't none of those guys a hundred percent straight."

"Not even Paco? I heard he has a wife back in Mexico."

"What the wife don't know don't hurt her," he said. "Not that I know personally. Nobody's giving it away to me for free these days, and I can't afford to pay. But I hear them talking, see men come and go. I ain't so old I've forgotten what a man looks like when he's eager and horny, and what he looks like after he's got his rocks off."

"You know what time it was on Saturday you saw Paco leave?"

He thought for a minute. "'Bout three, I think. Usually he rides his bike to work. Blue one, with purple Mardi Gras beads wrapped around the handlebars. He was gearing up when his friend showed up. You know his name?"

"Ricardo, I think."

"Ricardo pulls up in a big black SUV, loads Paco's

THE NEXT ONE WILL KILL YOU

bike in the back, then Paco gets in with him. Haven't seen him since."

"Thanks." I hesitated. "You need anything?"

"If it weren't for all these meds, I'd tell you what I needed," he said, cackling again. "Been a long time since a sweet-looking boy like you made me an offer."

I blushed.

"You go on," he said.

I handed him my card. "If you see anything," I said.

He took the card, turned around, and shuffled back into his apartment.

I went back to I-95 and headed south, dodging big rigs and slow-moving tourists. It seemed like it was always rush hour on the highway, no matter what time of day. There was always some hotshot darting between cars, eager to reach his destination an extra minute earlier, and more and more lately I saw cars moving slowly, their drivers intent on cell phones, either talking or texting. Made me think about switching my little Mini for a big honking SUV with side-impact air bags.

Following the directions on my phone, I got off the highway at Griffin Road and turned west, then made a quick left at the animal shelter. With my window down, I could hear the yips and barks of abandoned dogs desperate to find someone to love them.

I passed a lake filled with small sailboats, the water choppy in the light breeze, and then turned down a street that ran parallel to high-tension wires. To my right were block after block of manufactured homes, compact but nicely landscaped. It was a whole different side to Broward County, far from the pricey waterfront condos or the vast western suburbs of big houses in cul-de-sacs.

It started to rain lightly, the drops splattering against the windshield in what looked like tiny paw prints. The street dead-ended at the ME's office, a collection of single-story buildings and trailers next to a sheriff's station with a bomb squad truck parked in the driveway. By the time I pulled up it was closing in on five o'clock, but a morgue doesn't run on normal business hours.

It was my first time there, and I wasn't impressed, even though I knew the ME had handled some high-profile cases, including Anna Nicole Smith's death at the Seminole Hard Rock Hotel and Casino a couple of miles away. I darted from my car to the office, hurrying up a short wooden staircase.

I waited in the lobby for a few minutes until Maria Fleitas was free. She was a short Latina with shoulder-length dark hair, bangs, and funky red-framed glasses. She wore a lab coat with her name embroidered on the left breast over light-green scrubs. "Agent Green," she said. "You brought a picture of your guy?"

"Yup." I showed her the photo taken at the Labor Day party. "I'm looking for the round-faced guy in the middle."

"Well, you found him. Come on back."

I gulped. It was a big jump from thinking about Paco being dead to seeing his body. But if I was going to be an FBI agent, I would have to butch up now and then. So I did.

6
SKELETONS WITH TOE TAGS

Dr. Fleitas led me down a hallway decorated for Halloween, with paper ghouls and goblins. The plastic skeletons dangling from the ceiling all had toe tags. "Coroner humor," she said as we passed.

We ducked out the back door and hurried across to a refrigerated trailer. She swiped her ID badge to open the door, then led me through a small operating room. The smell was awful, and I nearly gagged. She handed me a tub of Vicks VapoRub and said, "Put some of this on your upper lip."

It helped, a little. I followed her through the room to a refrigerated cooler. She opened the door and bent down to check the ID on one bed-like shelf. Then she slid the shelf out and pulled down the sheet covering the face.

"This your Juan Doe?" she asked.

My stomach jumped as I looked down at Paco Gonzalez. His eyes were closed, his lips sealed tight, and his skin had a bluish tinge. There were vicious scratches up and down his plump face, and it looked like part of his cheek had been cut away.

Dr. Fleitas must have seen the look on my face. As she pulled on a pair of rubber gloves, she said, "Don't worry, the scratches on his face are postmortem. He was dead when he was dumped in the water, but as he was pushed down the canal his arms, legs, and face would have dragged against the bottom."

"He didn't float?"

She shook her head. "Bodies are heavier than water. Once he was tossed in the canal, he sank. His body started to decompose, releasing gasses. Eventually the gas caused him to rise to the surface." She pointed to his cheek. "See that? Scavenger. Once he'd been eaten away enough, or his body punctured enough to let the gas escape, he'd have sunk to the bottom again."

I focused on steadying my breathing as I compared the body to the photo. "Looks like he's my missing guy."

"Hercules Dumond will be happy to hear that."

"Who's he?"

"He's the BSO detective assigned to this case."

The Broward Sheriff's Office investigated crimes in unincorporated parts of the county, and had also swallowed up a lot of local police departments.

She picked up a notepad and scrawled a name and phone number. When she handed the page to me, I saw the logo of the Los Angeles County Coroner's gift shop at the top, along with the outline of a dead body and the slogan "We're dying for your business."

"You'll call him, won't you?" she asked. "None of this secrecy business?"

"I'll have to check with my boss and see what I can pass on," I said. "What else can you tell me?"

My stomach was still doing flip-flops. I had been to funerals, and seen corpses as part of my training at Quantico, but there was something so immediate, so visceral, about being in the autopsy suite. I hadn't known Paco, but I knew people who had, and his death had become my case. That made it much more personal.

She gently turned his head to the side. "Cause of death," she said, pointing to a hole in the back of his head. "Single gunshot fired at close range. I recovered fragments of a steel-jacketed hollow-point, most likely from a .38 caliber handgun."

"Execution-style," I said.

She nodded. "From the angle of entry it appears that the victim was on his knees and that the gunman stood behind him. Because the hollow-point bullet expands after impact, it was safer for the gunman and any bystanders—less chance of over-penetration."

I pulled out my notebook and started writing down information. If I focused on specific details, I could ignore the smell and the nausea. "Where was the body found?"

She looked at a sheet of paper. "A couple of recreational boaters spotted him floating in the canal running parallel to I-75, about a mile west of the boat ramp at marker thirty-five."

One Saturday a couple of weeks before, Jonas and I had gotten in my Mini Cooper and gone for a long drive west. I-75 was a broad, bland highway that shot across the belly of the state from one coast to the other, with broad vistas of saw grass prairies to either side. It was odd to be so close to urban Florida and yet see the horizon stretching for miles, broken only by the occasional hardwood hammock in the middle of the swamp.

But dead bodies floating in the canal were a clear reminder of how close civilization—or what passed for it in South Florida—really was.

"Can you estimate a time of death?" I asked, as she peeled her gloves off and led me from the room.

"Hard to pinpoint because it's unclear how long the body was in the water. But I'd say roughly seventy-two hours ago."

"So Saturday sometime?"

She nodded. "You know the last time anyone saw the victim? That would help."

"One of the neighbors saw him leaving for work with a friend, around three o'clock on Saturday, but he never made it to his job."

I followed her into a small office. "That helps me narrow the time," she said, sitting down at her desk. "Thanks." She turned to her computer and began typing.

"Did you run his fingerprints through IAFIS?" I asked. The Integrated Automated Fingerprint Identification System was the national fingerprint database maintained by the FBI.

"Not yet. He degloved, which means the outer layer of the epidermis sloughed off. We have access to a scanner if we can't make an ID of a corpse through normal means. Hercules asked for his prints, but we're backed up, so I haven't done it yet. You need his prints for your case?"

"I'm not sure he was who he said he was," I said. "Would be useful to know if he had a record, or an alias."

She nodded. "All right. I'll work on it and call both you and Hercules tomorrow."

I thanked her and walked out into the narrow hallway lined with ghoulish decorations. I opened the outside door to the smell of mud and negative ions. The rain had slowed to a misty drizzle, and I wished I could stand in a downpour and wash away all traces of the morgue. Instead, I shivered and got into my car.

When I was an accountant in Philadelphia, my dreams of an exciting job did not include identifying the dead. I didn't like the smell, the creepy plastic skeletons on the wall, or the presence of so many bodies. Thank God the FBI didn't normally investigate homicides, or I'd seriously consider changing agencies.

Before I left the parking lot, I called Roly and told him what I'd discovered. "The ME gave me the name of the BSO detective handling the homicide. Guy named Hercules Dumond."

"Here's a lesson for you in inter-agency cooperation. Paco's death is a homicide. Because the body was found in an unincorporated part of Broward County, that means BSO is the lead investigative agency. But because Paco was already involved with the Bureau, we maintain our own investigation. For right now, at least, if Dumond calls you, you tell him to talk to me," Roly said.

"Will do." I looked through the windshield up at the sky. Angry thunderheads were massing over the Everglades, getting ready to move east and deluge Fort Lauderdale.

"What are you going to do now?" Roly asked.

"One of Paco's neighbors saw him leave on Saturday

afternoon with a guy named Ricardo, who used to work at Lazy Dick's. I want to track him down."

"All right. Check back with me tomorrow."

I hung up as a clap of thunder shook the car. I needed to get moving to outrun the storm but I wanted to make a couple more calls before I got on the road. As I dialed the number for Lazy Dick's, a flock of blue herons swooped past, fleeing the oncoming wind and rain. "Can I talk to Barry please?" I asked whoever it was who answered.

I sat on hold while Barry Weiner pulled Ricardo's job application. The palm trees bent in the wind, and pebbles from the driveway pinged against the trailer and the side of my car. "His last name is Lopez," he said, when he came back on the line. "Only address I have is the one with the other guys."

Did I believe Usnavy, that Ricardo had moved out? The neighbor had backed up that story. But where had he gone? Considering how many Lopezes there were bound to be in South Florida, it would be tough to find him.

I thanked Barry and hung up, then pressed one of the favorites on my phone. "Hey," I said. "You want to split some fried chicken with me?"

"Sure," Jonas said. "I think we've still got some beer left in the fridge."

I snapped the phone shut. A couple of beers in him, and Jonas would tell me everything he knew about the Mexicans working at Lazy Dick's. Probably more than I wanted to know.

7
A REGULAR FBI GUY

Jonas was sitting on the sofa in the living room when I walked in. "Dude," he greeted me.

"Dude." I decided I wouldn't waste time with preliminaries. "You know these guys?" I asked, showing him the photo. He looked at it while I dropped the bucket of chicken on the table along with my briefcase. The chicken smell had permeated my car and removed almost every trace of my visit to the morgue. I was even starting to feel hungry.

"Yeah. So?"

"So Paco's dead. And I'm trying to figure out why."

He looked up at me, and his face was pale. "Dead? But he was such a sweet guy." He picked up the photo and peered at it, as if there were some kind of aura around Paco that indicated he would die soon.

"Did you fuck him?"

"Not my type. He was strictly gay for pay, and I haven't sunk that low yet." He pushed the picture back to me. "How come the FBI is handling a homicide? And why you? I thought you were a number-cruncher."

"I'm a special agent, just like the rest of the guys," I said, pulling off my tie. "Well, maybe a little more special than most. Remember how I told you those other agents from my office were at Lazy Dick's on Saturday? They were there to meet with Paco. But he never showed up. So I got tasked with finding him."

I pulled a Sea Dog Raspberry Wheat from the refrigerator. I like fruity beers. Go figure. Then I sat down across from Jonas. "I found him today. At the morgue."

"But why aren't the regular cops doing this?"

I took a long pull from my beer. I could taste the sweetness of the raspberries underneath the crispness of the ale. I was hoping the alcohol would wipe away the last traces of the morgue, though I had a feeling I'd remember Paco's scratched and bloated face for a long time.

"Until I identified him about an hour ago, he was a Juan Doe, so there wasn't much the local cops could do. I'll have to interface with them tomorrow."

"Listen to you. Tasked. Interface. You talk like a regular FBI guy."

"Which I am." I reached for a chicken breast, and inhaled the fragrance of all those special spices. "Which brings us back to what you know about Paco."

He shrugged. "Nothing. Just enough to say hey to him at the bar."

From the way he wouldn't meet my eyes, I knew Jonas was hiding something. I tried to remember the interrogation techniques I'd been taught. We'd had sessions on "elicitation"—the ability to get information without seeming to. One of those ways was to be a good listener, to exploit people's instincts to complain or brag. So I waited and listened.

I took a bite of the chicken: crispy on the outside, juicy on the inside. Damn, it was good.

I pushed the bucket toward Jonas. "And?"

"And nothing."

I looked from Jonas to the photo and back again. There was something there. But what? And then I knew. "What about this other guy? Ricardo."

"We had sex. Once. No big deal."

I put the breast down on a paper napkin. "Jonas. You paid him? You just said you hadn't sunk that low."

"We fooled around, and then he said he needed some money to send home, so I gave him fifty bucks. It wasn't like he was a prostitute or anything."

I shook my head. "What's wrong with you, dude? You're not ugly, you're not an old troll or anything. You have a look that a lot of guys like. Why do you need to pay for sex?"

"Says Mr. Gorgeous," he said. "You never even have to pay for a drink at the bar. Not everybody has your cute face or your bubble butt."

It was Jonas's same old song, but I didn't have the patience for his self-pity. "What do you know about Ricardo?" I asked, picking up the chicken breast again and taking another big bite. "I heard he got fired for mouthing off at work."

"I don't know. He was okay with me. We partied, shared a little coke."

"Jonas. You didn't bring coke into this house, did you?

Fuck, man, I could lose my job if the cops ever found coke where I live."

"Not here. The restroom at Lazy Dick's. And I know, you're Mr. Straight Arrow. I wouldn't bring anything into the house, or even in my car if you were riding with me."

I took a deep breath. It wasn't the time to start yelling at Jonas. "Last time anybody saw Paco, Ricardo was picking him up on Saturday afternoon."

Jonas picked up a chicken leg and bit into it. "Gotta love the Colonel," he said.

"Yeah. Listen, you have any way to get in touch with Ricardo?"

"I have his cell number. Don't know if it still works or not."

"I think it's time for a booty call." I spotted Jonas's phone on the coffee table, got up, and retrieved it, all while destroying the chicken breast in my hand. "Go for it, dude. Your country needs you."

"Angus," he whined.

I didn't say anything, just looked at him and kept eating my chicken.

"Whatever." He picked up the phone, scrolled through the contacts, and pressed a couple of buttons. He held the phone toward me, so I could hear as it rang, then went to voice mail.

Jonas glared at me, then said into the phone, "Hey, Ricardo, it's Jonas. I was thinking of you and remembering how we hooked up after Labor Day. I'm kind of hot and bothered and was hoping you could come over here and make it all right. Call me."

He hung up.

"That's your best line?" I asked. "No wonder you have to pay for sex."

"Fuck you, Angus." He tossed the chewed-up bone in the trash and picked out another leg.

We ate the rest of the chicken in silence, and then Jonas went into his room, probably to jack off to computer porn. "Let me know if he calls you," I said, to his back.

I called Danny's cell, but his voice mail picked up. "I'm going out later," I said. "E-mail or text me if you need something ASAP."

When Ricardo hadn't called by ten o'clock, I walked up to Jonas's door, knocked and asked, "You want to go to Lazy Dick's?"

"Fuck you," he said, without opening the door.

I tried the handle. It was locked. "Come on, Jonas. Come with me."

"Just fuck off, Angus."

I could get him to open the door if I promised to suck him—but I wasn't prepared to go that far in search of information.

"Fine. See you later."

I took my time getting dressed, making a lot of noise in the living room, hoping Jonas would relent, but he stayed in his room. I remembered what Vito had reminded me of on Saturday night—that it was good policy to carry my gun even when I was off duty. I had to figure out what I could wear to Lazy Dick's that would cover up the holster on my belt, because I sure wasn't wearing a jacket when it was still in the eighties even at night.

I picked a short-sleeved cotton shirt I could wear with the tails out and a pair of cargo shorts. It was close to eleven by the time I made it to the bar, which was pretty lively for a Monday night. I stopped in the parking lot for a moment, looking at the neon dry cleaner's sign across the way. I'd come clean as an FBI agent to Raj, Barry Weiner, and the kitchen staff, plus Helen Wheels. Knowing the way gossip spreads, I was worried that when I walked in, every head would turn to look at me.

But it was just another night at Lazy Dick's, and the older crowd, mostly retired guys along with a few twinks looking for free drinks, didn't pay any attention to me. I wondered if that was the way the older men saw me, too—as a cute, brainless young guy who flaunted his good looks.

I knocked on Barry Weiner's office door and got no answer. So I prowled around the bar looking for him, finding him in the men's room unstopping a toilet.

"Hand me that roll of paper towels, will you?" he asked.

I did. "Anybody here who was particularly friendly with Ricardo Lopez?" I asked. "I'm trying to track him down."

"First Paco, then Ricardo," he said.

"Yeah, well, I found Paco. At the morgue. And the last guy he was seen with was Ricardo."

He blanched. "You're serious?"

"Yup. Time to advertise for a new busboy."

"You're a hard bastard," he said.

I realized I'd been too flip. "If I didn't care what happened to Paco I'd be back home in bed. Or out front looking for someone to share that bed with me."

"Ricardo didn't leave here on the best of terms," Barry said. "Got into a catfight with one of the customers, and I had to let him go. I heard he moved out of the apartment he was living in right after that."

I moved around the bar, asking each of the busboys and waiters if he knew where Ricardo had gone. None of them had a clue, though two of them gave me his cell phone number—the same one Jonas had. None of them seemed bothered by the fact that I was an agent.

I walked up to the bar and before the bartender could come over, a fifty-something bear said, "Hey, handsome. Can I buy you a drink?"

"Thanks, but I'm not staying," I said.

"Whatever." He turned away from me.

I was getting fed up with attitude. Maybe it was the long day, or maybe something Jonas had said had hit home. I tapped the bear on the shoulder. "Excuse me," I said. "I'm not trying to diss you, pal. I'm just not here to get laid. If I was, then maybe you and I could have a couple of drinks together and get to know each other in a personal kind of way." I opened my wallet and flashed him my badge. "But I'm working here. All right?"

He looked as surprised as if I'd slapped him in the face. "Sure. Sorry. Don't let me get in your way."

The bartender came over. Raj was off duty, and Kyle, the young blond, was his replacement. "Hey, Angus," he said.

"Hey. You remember a busboy named Ricardo, quit about a month ago?"

"Sure."

"He say anything to you about where he was going? Back to Mexico? Some other bar or restaurant?"

He shook his head. "All I know is that he had a deal going with some cousin of his, gonna land him on Easy Street." He shrugged. "But half the guys in this bar are looking for that. Hell, more than half."

I thanked him, and turned back to the bear. "Take care of yourself, handsome," I said. I leaned over and kissed his cheek, grizzled with a five o'clock shadow, then walked out to my car.

Jonas was still locked in his room, probably asleep, when I got home. I checked my e-mail and found a message Danny had composed about his visit from the cops. He was asked a lot of questions about how he handled credit cards—did he run them through right away? Did he hold onto them, put them down somewhere?

Then the cops had asked a lot of prying questions about Danny's income and his spending habits. They threatened to get subpoenas for his bank records, and he was worried that they'd see the money he was saving up for Italy and think it came from theft.

I wrote back to him. I reassured him that the cops would be able to see that the big deposits had come from me, and that they'd be looking for large amounts, not a few dollars here and there. I promised that I'd talk to him again soon, and told him to call me if the cops came back.

8
FINGERS IN MANY PIES

The next morning, Jonas was in the kitchen pouring himself a glass of milk when I walked in. "He never called me." He put the bottle of milk back in the fridge.

"Listen, Jonas, I…."

"It's all right," Jonas said, but I could see that it wasn't. He took his glass of milk and went back into his bedroom, closing the door behind him.

When I got to work, I put in a request for Paco's Social Security records, based on the number he had put on his application at Lazy Dick's. Since Paco was usually just a nickname, the records should give me his real first name, too. I wanted to verify that he had actually worked at the convention center, and see if I could track down more information about him from any of his old coworkers.

I began to write up what I had learned on a form FD302, the standard field report. I'd already filled out way too many of them in my brief tenure with the Bureau. I recorded everyone I'd spoken to and everything I'd learned. Late in the morning I got a notification that my request for Social Security information for Francisco Gonzalez had come in through e-mail.

"This can't be right," I said out loud as I scanned through the report. Sure, it was a common name, but I was baffled by how many results had appeared. I started to dial Roly's number, but then hung up. This was one I was going to figure out by myself.

I started with the date of birth registered to that Social Security number: April 11, 1964. That didn't match the Paco whose body was in the morgue; he was nowhere near that old. He was more like twenty-five. And yet, that was the number Paco had given at Lazy Dick's.

At the academy, we'd learned that one of the most common ways of establishing a false identity was to assume the profile of someone who died as an infant. Find a likely subject, then request a copy of his birth certificate. Use that to apply for a driver's license, a replacement Social Security card, and so on.

But that would mean the real Francisco Gonzalez was dead. I looked back at the place of birth: Houston, Texas. I called up the Bureau of Vital Statistics for the state of Texas online, and did a search. There were enough men of that name to fill a Cuban baseball team, but I narrowed my search to the few years following the birth date on the records, and after hunting through a dozen screens, I found what I had been looking for.

The baby who had been born on April 11, 1964 and christened Francisco Gonzalez had died on November 10, 1966, also in Houston. But he had begun working in

1981, at a fast-food restaurant in Katy, Texas. And what an employee he had turned out to be! He had worked, often simultaneously, at jobs all across the state of Texas, from an oil refinery in Port Arthur to a dry cleaner's in Brownsville to a drugstore in Austin.

He was still working in Texas, at one restaurant in Killeen and another in Corpus Christi as well as an ice cream parlor in Galveston.

The reward for all this searching was to discover that one of the Pacos had worked for a concessionaire called Food Group International at the Miami Beach Convention Center. That was enough of a connection for me between the dead man and the convention center, validating the tip Paco had given to Roly over the phone. I realized that, though I'd looked at the photos and plans Navillus Sullivan had showed me, I'd never been to the center in person. Time to change that.

I called Sullivan and made plans to meet him the next day at the center for a walk-through. Then I called Dr. Fleitas at the morgue.

"It took some work, but I got a couple of decent prints," she said. "Ran them through AIFIS and got a hit, along with a report of criminal activity. I was just about to e-mail the results to you and Hercules."

I thanked her, and after a couple of minutes the fingerprints and the accompanying criminal report came in.

He had been born in La Tijerita, a small town in Mexico in Tamaulipas, about a half hour south of Matamoros, which was just across the Rio Grande from Brownsville, Texas.

At eighteen he had been arrested for petty theft in

Brownsville. Because he was an illegal alien, he had been sent back to Mexico almost immediately.

At some point, however, he had returned to the United States and moved to South Florida. Was he, as most people had said, a good guy? I'd read enough news stories to appreciate the desperation of many immigrants, so perhaps he'd been a Mexican Jean Valjean, stealing bread to feed his family.

For his call to the FBI tip line, he had probably used a beater cell phone—a disposable one that couldn't be traced. Did using an untraceable number show that he was smart? Or was a prepaid cell the only kind he could afford on his wages as a busboy?

Why have the agents come to the restaurant where he worked? Did Paco think he was slick enough to slip them something without anyone else noticing? Or maybe, since he got around on a bicycle, he simply couldn't come up with anywhere else to meet?

The fact remained that he had a criminal history, and was working under stolen credentials. But what had made him decide to contact the FBI? And was it that call which had gotten him killed—or because he knew too much about whatever was planned for the convention center?

The last person to see him was his former roommate and coworker, Ricardo Lopez. Did Ricardo know that Paco had a rendezvous with Bureau agents planned for that night? No one had seen Paco since the old man at the complex saw him get into Ricardo's SUV.

Had Ricardo killed him? Where was Ricardo? If he was still in Fort Lauderdale, he might be hanging around gay bars, looking to pick up sympathetic tricks like Jonas. But before hitting the bars, I hit the Internet, beginning with the hook-up invites on craigslist. Ricardo was a millennial like me, so he was probably tech-savvy.

I scanned through the past week of postings on Craig's List. A lot of guys out there were looking for some hot man-on-man action, but none of them matched what I knew of Ricardo Lopez. The same was true of Grindr. I saw a couple of guys I recognized from Lazy Dick's and messaged them about Ricardo. All I got in return were invitations for various sexual activities. I declined them all politely and logged off.

I called Jonas. "I need a wingman," I said. "Want to do a bar crawl with me?"

"You don't need me to help you hook up," he said.

"I'm not trying to hook up. I'm looking for Ricardo. Make yourself pretty and be ready in a half hour." I hung up before he could argue, and drove home.

He'd combed his hair, shaved, and put on a clean shirt, which was about as much prettying up as Jonas could manage. I figured he wasn't mad at me anymore for making him call Ricardo. I rocked the untucked look again to cover up my holster.

I had made a list of every gay bar in Broward County. There were twenty-four, which meant we couldn't spend too much time in any one. We started at a Levi's-and-leather bar in Fort Lauderdale. I showed Ricardo's picture to the bartender and each of the twelve customers around the bar. No one recognized him, though a few guys said they'd like to meet him if I found him.

By the third bar, Jonas was getting restless. "I want a drink. And I want to do some cruising."

"Really, Jonas?" We were at a piano bar catering to older

men. A couple of them were standing around a black baby grand singing along to "New York, New York." "You want to hang around here?"

"Not here. Can't we go to Lazy Dick's?"

"I've already gotten everything I can from the staff there. I tell you what, the next one on my list is Equinox. We'll have a drink there."

"I can deal with Equinox." It was a decent bar, too far from where we lived to make a habit of, but it had a great light show behind the bar and a tasty clientele. I drove south to State Road 84, a multi-lane road lined with run-down warehouses and discount gas stations, and pulled into the lot of a large concrete building illuminated by colored uplights along the walls. The sign out front was purported to be an equinox, the sun closing in on the moon, but if you looked closely you could see two testicles, with a giant flagpole and rainbow flag rising up between them.

We parked in the lot next to the tattoo parlor, beneath a large graphic of a sexy dude with tats of colored swirls. From the outside, Equinox gave off a more hard-edged vibe than Lazy Dick's, and I could almost smell the testosterone in the air, under the aromas of beer and sweat.

A dark-haired muscle-bound hunk, at least six-four and bulging like Schwarzenegger, checked our IDs at the door, and we headed for the bar, an oblong island beneath a rack of overhead lights. House music pounded in our ears, and over on the dance floor a half-dozen guys danced by themselves.

Jonas and I walked up to the bartender, a twenty-something dude with a scruffy beard and a brown man bun, wearing a skin-tight tank top that emphasized every muscle in his upper body. I bought Jonas a Heineken and ordered a Coke for myself. The bartender uncapped the beer and drew the Coke from the dispenser, and as he came back over to us I showed him my badge and the photo of Ricardo. "Recognize this guy?" I asked, leaning forward so he could hear me.

He picked up the photo and shifted so he could see it better. "Yeah, he comes in sometimes."

"Really? Remember the last time he was here?"

He frowned, which made it look like he was thinking, and I wanted to apologize. He probably didn't do that much. "Sunday night," he said. "He got into a fight with another dude. Lester had to make them leave."

He nodded across the room, to the guy who'd checked our IDs.

I thanked him and left him a ten. I told Jonas I'd be back, picked up my Coke, and walked over to the big, sexy bouncer, Lester.

As I approached him, I couldn't help considering what he'd be like in bed. I'm six foot one and on the slim side, and ever since I had joined the FBI, my taste in men had been tending toward guys bigger than me. Maybe it was some subconscious thing, looking for someone who could protect me when I was off duty. Or maybe I just liked being wrapped up in hefty biceps.

I swallowed hard and willed my dick to soften. "Angus Green, FBI," I said, showing Lester my badge. "Can I talk to you?"

He looked me up and down. "Don't get many G-men around here."

"Who knows, maybe I'll make this place a regular

hangout." I couldn't help myself; I smiled. "The bartender said you broke up a fight on Sunday night."

He flexed his shoulders, and I had to work to keep my tongue in my mouth. I gave up on the hard-on. It was tenting my khakis and yearning its way toward Lester.

I showed him the picture. "Yeah, that's the guy," he said. "Your boyfriend?"

"Not in this life," I said.

"How about the dude at the bar?"

"Just a roommate." I swallowed again. "So what can you tell me about what happened?"

He looked at the picture again. "He drove a black Toyota SUV," he said. "With a funky decal on the back. The Mexican flag, but a strange shape. Got a pen?"

I pulled one out of my pocket and handed it to him. My fingers tingled as they connected with his. He sketched the detail on the back of the photo. "Looks like a Maltese cross," I said.

"If you say so."

"Anybody with him?"

"Nah. He was cruising. Didn't get lucky here."

He looked over at the bar, where Jonas was deep in conversation with a blond guy who looked a lot like me. "Looks like your roommate's going to get some tonight, though," he said. "How about you?"

Something about Lester rocked my world, and I was interested to see what the aftershocks would be like. "That depends." I looked Lester in the eye. "I've got a day job, so I can't stay out too late. You working until closing?"

Lester licked his lips. "My replacement will be here at midnight."

"I've got to hit a couple more bars, looking for this guy. But I'll be back by then."

"I'll be waiting."

My dick was pulsing so hard against my pants that it was clear it didn't want to wait, but that was just tough. I checked back in with Jonas, told him I was going to keep moving around and be back at Equinox by midnight. That was fine with him.

I circled through a half dozen parking lots, looking for a black SUV with a Mexican flag decal in a Maltese cross shape. No luck. I showed Ricardo's picture to bartenders and patrons, and no one recognized him. I was feeling discouraged until I remembered that Lester was waiting for me, and made my way back to Equinox.

And there he was, standing by the front door talking to a black guy almost as big as he was. "Your roommate told me to tell you he'd get home on his own," Lester said.

"That's good news," I said.

"Here's even better news," Lester said. "I'm off the clock. I've just got to get my stuff from the back."

He reached out and took my hand in his. His grip was strong and cool and sent vibrations direct to my dick. "Come on, G-man. Let's see what kind of trouble we can get into."

9
GATHERING INFORMATION

It was early morning before I left Lester's apartment, which meant I was operating Wednesday on only a few hours' sleep, and my body ached in some very awkward places. I settled into my office chair, squirmed around until I found a comfortable angle, and turned on my computer.

There was no message from Danny, either on my phone or in my e-mail. What was up with that idiot? Call me with a big crisis, then never follow up? I thought about reaching out to him again, but it was too early in the morning. He usually worked at La Scuola until two, then scrambled to make his first class at ten.

I opened up Danny's e-mail and read through it again. La Scuola relied on turnover, and the owner was cheap, so servers were always busy. I couldn't imagine one of them having the time to write down fifteen-digit card numbers, expiration dates, and verification numbers along with the name on the card.

I remembered something I'd learned while helping out with a fraud case in Philadelphia. A store clerk at a big mall had used a tiny device called a skimmer to capture information from the magnetic stripe on customer credit cards. He had then sold the information to someone online, who had used the data to create counterfeit cards. In turn, those cards were passed on to people who used them to buy stuff, often prepaid gift cards, which could then be sold legitimately.

Since the purchases were usually fairly small—a batch of low-value cards, the occasional hundred-dollar ones—no alert was triggered by the card company, and the customers didn't discover the problem until they received big surprises on their next statements.

Was someone doing the same thing at La Scuola? I pulled up a couple of pictures of skimmers online and e-mailed them to Danny, asking if he'd seen anyone use something like that around the restaurant.

I hadn't found Ricardo the night before, but Lester had told me Ricardo drove a black Toyota SUV. I pulled the registration for every matching vehicle in Broward County, hoping he hadn't changed his registration when he moved. I compared the results I found to the address where Ricardo had lived with Paco and the other guys from Lazy Dick's.

Bingo. Ricardo Lopez, of that address, owned a 2008 Toyota RAV4 in black.

I thought about contacting the BSO detective Dr. Fleitas had told me was investigating Paco's murder. I could ask him to put out a BOLO for Ricardo's SUV based on the plate number I had. But I didn't want the cops to get to Ricardo before I did, because I wanted answers to my questions first.

I left the office a few minutes later for the drive down to Miami Beach and my appointment with Navillus Sullivan. It was a gorgeous day for a drive, a yellow sun shining in a sky so blue it made my eyes hurt. I slipped a Springsteen CD into the dash, got on I-75, and began singing along with the Boss. I had my own case, I had sources to interview and a property to check out.

I just had to remember that this had all begun with a dead man.

The miles passed quickly, and I turned onto the Julia Tuttle Causeway, my favorite road in all of Miami. It ran across Biscayne Bay, with sparkling blue, green, and turquoise water on both sides. Sailboats dotted the bay, and fishermen stood by the roadside casting their lines.

I felt great. I'd had terrific sex the night before, and it was the kind of beautiful day I'd only daydreamed of back in Pennsylvania. I had to wait for the light at the highway exit, next to a beat-up old station wagon with rows of garishly colored plastic dragons glued to the bumper, the hood, and the roof. When I looked over to check out the driver, a grizzled older man, I saw a stuffed purple dragon belted into the passenger seat. You just didn't see stuff like that in Scranton.

I parked in the garage across from the convention center and met Navillus Sullivan at the entrance to Hall C. He wore a beige guayabera, a Cuban shirt with multiple pockets across the front, which hung loose over his waist. I figured that meant he had a gun underneath. Mine was hidden by my suit coat.

"The dealers will valet park," Sullivan said, pointing to the stand in front of the building. "None of them want to be wandering around parking lots or garages carrying briefcases full of jewelry."

"The valets are bonded?" I asked.

He nodded.

"How secure is the lot they use?" I asked. "If these guys are well-organized they can target a distributor's rental car as he drives in and watch where the valet parks."

"Hide in the car all day?" Sullivan said. "Too hot."

"They'd have another man in the building following the distributor," I said. "Radio to the outside man with enough time for him to place himself in the vehicle."

"Possible," Sullivan said. He made a note. "Usually the distributors are savvy enough to check the car before they get in, but we'll be sure to include that warning in the materials we hand out."

Sullivan had a map of the center, and we spent the next two hours walking the entire building, surveying entrances and exits, kitchens, and loading docks. I wished I had the map Paco had drawn for Ricardo; it would have been interesting to see what he'd found worth noting.

I pulled out my notebook. "Our informant worked for a company called Food Group International," I said. "Are they the main concessionaire here?"

"A number of companies work here, depending on the show," Sullivan said. "FGI is one of the big ones. They man the pushcarts that sell snacks, coffee, and water, and they operate a sit-down café in each of the halls."

"Let's focus on them," I said. "Our informant may have found a security breach somewhere."

We stopped at one of the FGI carts and got a couple bottles of water, and continued our search. We saw where the carts were stocked and where they were stored and examined the loading dock behind each café. "What about the employees? Who vets them? The convention center? Or the individual concessionaire?"

"The concessionaires. Each employee gets a plastic passcard that they use to swipe in and out of the employee entrance, so we know who's in the building at all times."

I shook my head. "I wasn't asking about access. What about criminal records?"

"It's up to the employer if they're willing to hire someone with a record. The kind of people who are willing to work for minimum wage…." He shrugged. "Let's just say you don't get Ivy League graduates."

I made a note that there could be a vulnerability associated with the food vendors. I wasn't sure what that could be, but it merited some more investigation. Paco had worked for the food service company, and it was possible that the map he had drawn for Ricardo had something to do with access to the food served to patrons. Could you put something like E. coli bacteria into the food and cause a mass poisoning? But what purpose would that serve?

Sullivan and I walked back toward the garage. I'd gotten a couple of ideas from our walk-through but I was reluctant to let Sullivan go without getting as much out of him as I could. "I could use a cup of coffee," I said. "Got a couple of minutes?"

He agreed, and as we walked toward the Starbucks on Lincoln Road, I asked, "If you were looking for a weakness at the convention center, where would you target?"

"If I found a weakness, I'd strengthen it," he said.

"Come on, Navillus. Work with me here. What's the weak link in the system?"

We dodged traffic on Seventeenth Street and walked down an alley next to the parking garage. The contrast between the glare on the street and the shade in the alley was startling, and reminded me that even in a sunny place like Miami Beach there could be dark corners. Sullivan sighed. "The weak link is not usually in the system. It's in the human capital."

I held the door to the coffee shop open for him and followed him to the counter. While we waited I asked, "What do you mean by human capital?"

"The people in the box office who sell the tickets. The security guards at the door. The delivery guys who bring in the merchandise and set up the displays. The models who show off the goods and look pretty. Each and every one of them is a point of vulnerability."

We stepped up to the counter and I asked, "What can I get for you?"

"Grande iced skinny vanilla latte with two Splenda," he said to the barista.

"And a venti chocolate chip frappucino," I added.

Sullivan shook his head. "I wish I had your metabolism. Hell, I wish I had the metabolism I had when I was your age."

We stepped down to the end of the counter to wait for our drinks, and I asked, "Do you get a list of all those personnel?"

He shook his head. "We don't credential part-time and short-term employees before the show. So all the delivery people, no. And pretty much anybody in a uniform from a delivery company comes and goes at will. Ditto anybody in a police or fire uniform. We issue badges to the people who work directly for the center, and the people who get credentialed for the individual shows."

We retrieved our drinks and sat down at a table in the corner. "Sounds like a lot of people to keep track of."

He nodded. "Our focus is on prevention. Security cameras, metal detectors, credentialing, controlling points of access. A determined thief or terrorist is still going to find a way in. Look at 9/11. Who had thought of commandeering a plane to crash it into a building before Osama bin Laden did it?"

I thanked Sullivan for his help and told him I'd be in touch, and as I drove back to the office I used the voice recorder on my cell phone to dictate everything that I had learned. When I got to my desk, I transcribed it all, adding in details like a link to a map of the convention center. It was nearly seven o'clock by the time I was finished.

I drove home, hoping to talk to Jonas about Ricardo Lopez, but he wasn't there. Figured. Just when I wanted to talk to the guy, he was off somewhere. When I wanted to be on my own, he was underfoot.

I was excited about the progress my case was making. I couldn't sit still, so I vacuumed the living room and my bedroom, moving the furniture around, finding things we'd lost weeks before. I called Danny and left another message, asking if he'd seen the e-mail about the skimmer. By nine o'clock I was tired and sweaty but filled with a sense of accomplishment.

Then my cell phone rang. I didn't recognize the number. "Green."

"Angus? It's Lester."

My mood got even better with those couple of words. "Hey, bud. How's it going?"

His voice was low. "That guy you were looking for? He's here in the bar."

"Ricardo?"

"If that's his name. Skinny Mexican dude. I checked the parking lot just to be sure. That same SUV with the funky flag decal is there."

"Shit. All right. Keep an eye on him. I'm on my way."

10
HARD ACT TO FOLLOW

I ran into my bedroom, kicking off my shorts as I dialed Roly's cell phone. I was tearing through my bureau drawers looking for something to wear when the call went right to voice mail. Shit.

"Roly, it's Angus. That guy Ricardo, the one who picked up Paco at his apartment? He's at Equinox, a gay bar on State Road 84. I'm on my way over there now. Call me when you get this."

I pulled on skimpy shorts that showed off my legs, and a pair of sneakers without socks, along with an oversized Florida State T-shirt of Jonas's. It hung loosely enough over my waist that I could slip my Glock into its quick-release holster.

It was wrong to go running into Equinox myself. I'd have to stake out the parking lot, keeping an eye on Ricardo's Toyota, until Roly called me. Then I remembered Vito. I didn't have his cell number, though.

I stopped halfway out the door, took a deep breath. Lester was keeping an eye on Ricardo. I had to take things slowly. I scrambled over to my laptop, turned it on, and logged into the FBI database. My fingers shaking with nervous energy, I scrolled and clicked until I found Vito's information. Fortunately, he lived in Fort Lauderdale himself; if I could get hold of him he could meet me at Equinox.

I dialed his home number. "Hello?" The voice was young and babyish.

"Can I speak to your dad, please?" I asked.

"You mean my husband," the voice said, with an unpleasant edge. "Hold on."

"Mastroianni. Who's this?"

"Angus. Angus Green. The guy we're looking for is at the bar. I got a call. At Equinox, in Wilton Manors."

"Slow down, rookie," he said. "Take a deep breath. What guy are we looking for?"

I did as he said, taking the time to formulate my thoughts. "I got a call from the bouncer at Equinox. He's at the bar now, and spotted the guy who picked up your informant Paco Saturday afternoon."

"Good work. I'll meet you there. Fifteen minutes? What's your cell?"

We traded numbers, and I hung up. I jumped into my car and headed toward Equinox. As I was pulling into the parking lot, looking for Ricardo's SUV, Danny called me.

"Danny, this isn't a good time. I'm working," I said.

"Shit, man. You're always blowing me off."

"I'm sorry, Danny." I looked around and spotted Ricardo's SUV. That meant he was still in the bar, and I couldn't do anything until Vito showed up. "Did you get my e-mail?"

"Yeah. But I've never seen anything like that. Angus, a cop came to my dorm this afternoon."

"What happened?"

"He kept pressing me, like he was sure I was the one responsible, and he was going to find out eventually, so why didn't I just tell him and get it over with." He started to cry. "I didn't do anything, but he's going to arrest me and put me in jail."

"He can't arrest you without evidence," I said. "And if you didn't do anything wrong, there won't be any evidence for him to find. Right?"

Danny didn't say anything, just sniffled.

Christ. Was there a chance Danny was involved in this?

I was a hard act to follow. Schoolwork had come easily to me, and it was rare for me to get anything less than an A. I was so busy covering up my attraction to other boys that I never got in trouble. Never got detention, was never sent to the principal's office. I started working at sixteen, making my own money.

Danny was smart too, but he was lazy, and sometimes he did poorly in school just to differentiate himself from me. He was such a cute kid, and then a good-looking young man, that he got away with the occasional cheating on a test or adolescent prank.

Could he have stolen credit card numbers, though? I didn't think so, but I couldn't let my love for him blind me to the possibility.

"You know you're my dawg," I said. "Nothing you do or say can ever change the way I feel about you."

"I know, Angus," he said, still sniffling.

"So if there's something you need to tell me, just say it. I'll take care of you. I always have and I always will."

Guys were passing where I sat in the car, on their way into the bar to have fun. I wanted to be like them, instead of working a case and trying to handle my brother at the same time.

I took a deep breath. I hated to ask, but I had to. "Did you steal those credit card numbers?"

"Fuck you, Angus," Danny said. "You think I would do something like that?"

I didn't like the angry edge to his voice, but I forced myself not to respond to it. "I don't think you did. But I want you to know that if you ever get in trouble, real trouble, you can come to me."

"Whatever."

Vito's black Toyota hybrid pulled up in the parking lot.

"Listen, Danny, I've gotta go. But I want you to look around the restaurant for a little machine like the one I sent you the picture of. Keep your eye on the other servers."

"You want me to spy on my friends?" His tone was still angry.

"If someone at that bar is stealing from customers, he's not your friend," I said. "Call it spying, or call it just paying attention. But it's your ass on the line, bro. Do what you have to do to protect yourself."

Danny didn't sound convinced, but he said he'd look around. I ended the call and got out to meet Vito beside his car. "Your guy still inside?" Vito asked.

"His car's still here, and my contact didn't call to tell me he was leaving."

Vito looked me over. "You'll blend in there a lot better than I will. Go inside and see what he's up to, then call me."

11
LES IS MORE

Lester was standing just inside the front door when I walked in. "Hey," I said.

"Hey yourself. Your guy's over there by the pool table. In the blue shirt."

I looked across the room. The guy he pointed to was tall and skinny, with what looked like a deep tan. I pulled the photo out of my pocket and compared him to it. Yeah, that was Ricardo, though the camera had washed his skin out and made him look sallow. It had also exaggerated the acne scars, which didn't look so bad in real life.

His face was nothing spectacular, narrow like a fox's with a pointed chin, but he had a killer body, which hadn't been visible with other guys in front of him. Slim chest, narrow waist, and hips that were made for dancing. His tight jeans accentuated a big package.

But I wasn't there to fuck him—just to observe him and see how he fit into my investigation.

He was playing pool with an older guy, forties maybe, trim in a tough-looking way, with military-short hair and a twirly handlebar mustache. I stepped over to a quiet spot by the wall and called Vito. "He's here. How do you want to play this?"

"Let's see where he goes when he leaves the bar. There's two of us, so we should be able to tail him."

"Speaking of tail, what if he gets some? What if he doesn't go home?"

"Then we wait, rookie. Call me when he's starting to move."

I stuck the phone in my pocket and went back to Lester. "So I guess it's true what they say," I said.

"What's that?"

"That Les is more."

He smirked. "Took you all this time to make that one up?"

"Hey, I had a lot on my mind," I said. "Protecting the country and all."

"And who protects the protector?"

"I'm thinking it would take a big man," I said. "You up for the job?"

"We'll see. You leaving with me, or with him?" He nodded toward where Ricardo was still playing pool.

"Sadly, with him. For tonight."

"You should get a drink," Les said. "I think he's gonna be here for a while."

I ordered a virgin strawberry daiquiri, though I wouldn't have minded a little alcoholic relaxation. It was a pain to hang around a bar and be on duty, watching everybody else have fun. It was even more of a pain to know that I could be going home with Lester if I wasn't working.

That was not a piece of information I shared with Vito.

I realized as I waited for my drink that I was familiar with almost every gay bar in Fort Lauderdale, but I'd never been to a drinking establishment outside my own neighborhood, or one with a primarily straight clientele.

Was I ghettoizing myself? Did I need to make some straight friends? Make more of an attempt to socialize at work? I'd been living in a kind of bubble, first in college, then in Philadelphia, and now in Florida, where I surrounded myself with people like me. Was that the kind of life I wanted?

I picked up my drink and walked around the room, ending up back near the door with Lester. "So what's your story?" I asked. "How did you end up here?"

"You mean here by the door?" he asked. "Here at Equinox? Here in Florida?"

"All of the above. Though I figured out the door part by myself."

"Smart guy." He looked sideways at me. "Cute, too. I've always had a soft spot for redheads."

"Gee, last night it was pretty hard," I said.

He laughed. "Born in Lexington, Kentucky. My pop worked on a horse farm. Used to come home every night smelling like manure. That wasn't for me."

"Good call." I looked over at Ricardo. He had gotten a fresh beer and was drinking it pretty quickly. Turning back to Lester I said, "Football or basketball?"

"Both, in high school." He smiled. "Football was my favorite, though. The quarterback and I had a thing going."

I laughed. "Jeez, you're like a walking wet dream, aren't you? Handsome, sexy, and a jock to boot, with some hot locker room stories."

"Never in the locker room." He crossed his arms over his chest and looked away from me. I thought he was angry until I saw he was watching a drunk by the bar. "Back me up," he said.

He walked toward the bar. As we got there, I heard the bartender say, "I'm telling you, dude, I have to cut you off."

"You fucking prick," the drunk said. He was probably forty-something, but the cracked red veins in his nose and his general pallor made him look older.

"Time for you to go," Lester said, looming up next to the guy. Lester had six inches in height on him and a hundred pounds of muscle, but the drunk was already too far gone for rational thought.

"Fuck you, you muscle-bound, pin-dick moron," the drunk said.

Right on only one count. Lester was muscle-bound. But he was no pin-dick, and no moron either.

Lester took the guy gently by the arm. "Let's go, Paulie. Come on, I'll walk you out to the street." To me, he said, "Paulie's a good guy, just drinks too much. Fortunately he lives a couple of blocks away, so he doesn't have to get behind a wheel."

Paulie started to struggle, but Lester wrapped his beefy arm around the drunk's shoulders and pulled him close.

"Oh, Jesus, don't nobody ever hold me like that anymore," Paulie said, and he started to blubber.

"It's okay, Paulie. Come on, you'll feel better outside."

I watched as Lester steered Paulie through the crowd. Then I turned back toward the pool table to check on Ricardo.

He was gone.

Shit. I pulled my cell out and dialed Vito. "Ricardo come outside?" I asked.

"What, you lost him?" Vito asked. "Haven't seen him."

"All right, he must be in here somewhere." I ended the call before Vito could bitch at me. The bar was packed, and it was tough getting around, but I made a full circuit and couldn't see Ricardo anywhere. I squeezed over to the men's room and walked inside, assailed by the smell of urine, ammonia, and male sweat.

There was nobody at the urinal, but one of the stalls was occupied. I walked over to the urinal and started to pee, then heard something slam against one wall of the stall, followed by a moan.

I finished, shook off, and zipped up. Then I peered under the door of the stall.

There were two pairs of feet in there. I recognized the suede cowboy boots as belonging to the older man Ricardo had been playing pool with. The other guy worn green flip flops and had an Aztec tattoo on one ankle, but I hadn't noticed Ricardo's footwear or body art so I couldn't be sure it was him.

A young guy pushed open the door of the men's room as I was looking under the stall door. "Not cool, dude," he said.

I straightened up quickly, blushing. "I'm not… it's not…" I stammered.

"Yeah, right."

He stood there watching me as I washed my hands,

waiting for me to finish before stepping over to a urinal himself. "Go on, you're done here," he said. "This is not some kind of zoo where you can watch the animals."

I considered flashing him my badge, but that might make things worse, especially if he started yelling about entrapment. So instead I walked out of the men's room and looked around for either Ricardo or Lester.

No Ricardo. But Lester was back at his post by the door.

"Where's your guy?" Lester asked when I reached him.

"Not sure. Maybe the men's room." I told him about the two guys in the stall.

"Ricardo was wearing shorts," he said. "Didn't see what kind of shoes he had on."

We looked back to the men's room. "What the fuck are they doing in there?"

Lester laughed. "I could show you."

For the second time that night I felt my face redden. It's a curse of the fair-skinned, constant blushing. Or maybe it's just that I seem to do and say dumb things.

My phone rang. "You find him?" Vito asked.

"Not sure. I think he's in the men's room."

"What do you mean, you think? Go in and see."

"He's... uh... occupied," I said.

Lester nudged me, and I looked up. Ricardo was coming out of the men's room, pulling the belt on his shorts tight. "Got him," I said to Vito. "He's still here."

"Yeah, well, keep your eye on him," he grumbled.

"Will do."

I stuck the phone back in my pocket. Almost immediately, it rang again.

"You're a popular guy tonight," Lester said.

"It's just my brother." I felt guilty, but I let the call go to voice mail. "So. Last I recall you were fooling around with the quarterback, but not in the locker room." I had to admit the thought was making me hard, imagining a younger Lester with his football uniform around his feet, naked as he'd been the night before.

"Football scholarship to the University of Kentucky, but I never played first string," Lester said. "Majored in education, wanting to be a gym teacher, and spent most of my time in the weight room. Taught high school phys ed for a couple of years in the hill country and hated it. So I came down here last winter to get some sun, ended up staying."

Ricardo was back at the pool table, playing a game with someone else. If he had a pattern—pool and then party— Vito and I were in for a long night.

"How about you?" Lester asked. "You always want to be a G-man?"

I shrugged. "I majored in accounting at Penn State, got my master's, took a desk job in Philly. Like you, I hated what I was doing. Saw a sign in a bar that the FBI was hosting a meet-and-greet cocktail party with the local gay chamber of commerce, and I went, expecting they'd laugh and turn me away. But they didn't. As I started interviewing, I got more into it. Seemed like it was a cool way to use my skills and get out from behind that desk now and then."

"You carry a gun?" he asked.

I turned sideways and leaned against him. "Yes, I am glad to see you—but that's a gun on my belt."

He laughed. "I like you, Angus."

I was about to reply something similar when I looked over at Ricardo. He shot the eight ball into the side pocket, and the guys around the pool table jeered at him. As I watched, he drank the last of his beer and waved goodbye to them.

I pulled my cell out of my pocket and ignored the missed call notice. "He's heading out," I said to Vito.

"I'll take point," he said. "You follow me until he makes a turn. I'll go straight, you follow him. Then I'll circle around and pick up behind you."

My adrenaline rose. I'd studied tailing techniques at the academy but hadn't had to put them in practice before.

"I need one more favor," I said to Lester as I turned toward the door, following Ricardo. "Can you get that pool cue he was using and hold it for me? It's got his prints on it. Then I'll be in touch. I know I owe you."

"I plan on collecting," Lester said as I walked out the door.

12

NILADY CRUZ

I took my time walking out to my car, making sure that Ricardo didn't see me. I plugged in the Bluetooth for my cell phone and sat there as he pulled out and turned right, Vito following him.

Ricardo turned right at the light, and Vito went straight. I turned behind Ricardo. I had a feeling he was heading for I-95. In my rearview mirror, I saw Vito had made a U-turn and was now behind me. Ricardo was still heading west, picking up speed, weaving across lanes.

Without signaling, he swung onto the entrance ramp to I-95 south. My phone buzzed, and I pressed the speaker button.

"Drop back," Vito said. "Let me pick him up again for a while."

"All right." As Ricardo sped up, moving into the left lane, Vito got behind him. I moved to the right, trying to match them for speed.

All three of us were closing in on the county line when Ricardo swerved to the right at the Hallandale Beach Boulevard exit. As I followed him off the interstate, I heard Vito cursing, and in my rearview mirror I saw that he'd been cut off and couldn't get over in time.

"Let me know if he goes east or west," Vito said. "I'll pick you up when I get off."

"He's turning west," I said.

There was no traffic on the road, so I hung as far back from Ricardo's SUV as I could. The light ahead turned yellow, and I was worried he'd race through, but instead he slammed to a stop.

I slowed, creeping up behind him, willing the light to change.

"Fucking traffic," Vito said, through my car's speaker. "I'm on Ives Dairy Road heading west."

That was the next major road south of where we were. "We're just coming up to 441," I said. "Stopped at the light."

"I'm turning. Catch you soon."

The light changed, and Ricardo zoomed through the intersection, then slowed and turned right, into a residential neighborhood. "Right behind you," Vito said. "I'll follow him. You go one street farther west and turn."

"Will do."

As I made the turn, Vito said, "He's slowing; he's turning into a driveway. Meet me at the corner up ahead."

I rounded the corner and saw Vito's hybrid. I pulled up on the other side of the street, one house away. By the time I walked over to Vito's car, he was punching something into his cell phone.

"Take a walk," he said. "Then come back and tell me what you see."

It was closing in on 1:00 a.m., and the street was quiet. With Halloween coming, a couple of houses had carved pumpkins and ghostly sheets out. I tried to stay in the shadows, while at the same time walking like I knew where I was going.

Ricardo's SUV was in the driveway of a ranch-style house. No Halloween decorations. The yard needed a good mowing, the house a coat of paint. There were no lights on inside that I could see. It looked to me like Ricardo had come home.

At the corner I stopped and turned around. As I walked back to Vito's car, a low-rider cruised slowly past me, rap music booming out of the stereo. My heart rate quickened, but I forced myself to keep moving at the same rate. The car continued past me, turning at the next corner.

I stopped at Vito's car, and he rolled down the window. "I ran the address. Belongs to a woman named Nilady Cruz."

"Ricardo's last name is Lopez. Maybe it's his grandmother or aunt."

"Probably not a girlfriend, if he's hanging out at queer bars. I think I know that name. Hold on, let me do a search."

I stood next to his car as he typed something else into his phone. In the distance I heard that rap music and wondered if the car was going to come past again.

"Bingo," Vito said. "Knew I heard of her. She's a doctor from Cuba. She's come up in some intelligence actions."

"So what do we do?"

Vito turned the phone off. "I don't want to screw any other operation up by staking out the house tonight without a full look-see. This Cruz woman is involved in some serious shit."

We said goodnight, and as I walked back to my car, I called Lester. "It's Angus. Did you get that pool cue for me?"

"Yeah."

"Can I come over and pick it up?"

"I'm clocking out in about five minutes, and I'm sleeping in tomorrow morning," he said. "You come over to my place, you're staying the night."

"I can do that," I said.

When I got to Lester's, the pool cue Ricardo had used was on the kitchen table with a paper towel wrapped around it. I was pleased that Lester was sharp enough to have kept his own prints off it. I put it into a brown paper grocery bag, and then he collected on the favor I owed him.

We went to sleep spooned together. I woke at six and kissed his cheek as he slept, his big arms splayed out, a half smile on his face. I drove home with the pool cue by my side, then jogged five miles around the neighborhood before I jumped in the shower. Despite how little sleep I'd gotten in the past two days, I felt terrific.

I was still struggling to understand how Paco's drawing of the convention center connected to Ricardo Lopez. I was pretty sure Ricardo had killed Paco, most likely because he'd found out about Paco's call to the FBI tip line. Was Ricardo planning to rob someone at the show? That was a big jump—from server at a gay bar to jewelry thief.

If I watched Ricardo for a while, perhaps I could discover the connection, or identify who else he might be working with. I picked up a venti raspberry mocha and drove over to Nilady Cruz's house in Miramar, where Ricardo's SUV was still in the driveway. I parked up the street with a view of the house, slouched down in my seat, and sipped my coffee.

Traffic swirled around me. Moms loading school-bound kids in SUVs, men and women in business dress in everything from battered pickups to tricked-out low-riders. A statuesque Jamaican woman with her head wrapped in colorful cloth tottered past on high heels, walking a pair of floor-mop dogs. Haitian women in hotel uniforms walked down toward Miramar Parkway, where I imagined they would board buses. I was just getting to the bottom of my coffee when Ricardo came out of the house and got into his SUV.

I waited until he had backed out of the driveway to turn my car on. Then I watched as he pulled up at the stop sign at Miramar Parkway and signaled right.

He turned, and I followed, keeping a couple of car lengths behind him as he headed west. We crept through a couple of school zones and then he was on I-75, heading north. It was easier to follow him on the highway because there was so much other traffic.

It was harder once he got off at Griffin Road. I ended up right behind him at the traffic light, and had to keep my head down so he wouldn't notice me in his rear view mirror. He got into the left lane, and I stayed to the right, but fortunately he turned into a small warehouse complex.

I kept going, making a U-turn at the next light. His SUV was parked in front of an end unit with no signage.

I turned around, noted the address of the complex, and headed back to the office. Driving up to it always made me feel like a knight entering a medieval fortress. To my left was a single-story building where visitors were vetted before they were allowed to walk along a sidewalk to the main entrance. Our office and adjacent parking garage were surrounded by a tall white metal fence, and further isolated by retention ponds and marshes to control flooding and prevent a vehicle from crashing through the fence and getting up to the building.

I went directly to my office, and while I waited for my computer to boot up and connect to the network, I looked at the cue. It was a cheap one, about four feet long, made of aluminum, and the handle was scarred and dinged. I hoped it would hold a good set of prints.

Once I was able to sign on to the network, I opened a browser and found the website for the Broward County Property Appraiser. I accepted the terms of service and entered the address of the warehouse complex where Ricardo had stopped. I was writing down the information when Roly came in. "I spoke to Vito and he told me about your adventure last night. Sorry I didn't get back to you—I was on a surveillance of my own. Find anything out?"

As usual, he looked fresh and immaculate. His double-breasted dark suit had a very faint light-blue pinstripe, echoed in the color of his tie.

I nodded. "Vito and I tracked Ricardo Lopez to a house in Miramar registered to a woman named Nilady Cruz. Vito says she's come up in some other investigation, and he's following up on that." I took a deep breath. "This morning I staked out the house in Miramar, and I followed Lopez to a warehouse farther west."

"You followed him? On your own?" He crossed his arms over his chest.

"Yeah."

"That was a dumb move, Angus. He could have spotted you."

"I don't think he did."

He shook his head. "Even so. You should have had backup."

My disappointment must have shown on my face, because he relaxed his posture and said, "Consider it a lesson learned. What did you get?"

I turned my computer monitor toward him. "The warehouse where Ricardo went is owned by a company called WareCo. Can we trace them?"

"That name is familiar," Roly said. "Move over. Let me drive."

I stood up, and Roly sat down at my computer. He logged me out of the network and logged in as himself. "You think WareCo is part of an investigation?" I asked.

"Give me a minute." He kept typing, occasionally stopping to grunt a negative. "Not in any ongoing investigations," he said finally. "But why is the name familiar to me?"

"Someone you know personally?"

He shook his head. "No. Maybe…." He went back to typing. "Bingo. We had a guy from that company in our Citizen's Academy last year. Here's his name and e-mail address." He pointed to the screen.

The Citizen's Academy was a program the Bureau ran to educate civilians about our operations.

"I gave them a talk on the JTTF," Roly continued. "And this guy e-mailed me to ask some questions."

He picked up my phone and started dialing. "John Chen please," he said. "Special Agent Gutierrez from the FBI."

He drummed his fingers on my desk while he waited. "Hey, John, Roly. How've you been?" He listened. "Good, good. Hey, I've got a question about a warehouse on Griffin Road. WareCo's the owner."

He listened, then gave the guy on the other end of the phone the address. "Okay, sure, I'll hold." He put his hand over the receiver. "WareCo is the landlord. They own a lot of commercial property in south Broward. He's going to pull up the records for that unit."

I stood there, leaning against the wall, and waited with Roly.

"Yeah, thanks, John. Okay." He wrote down some information. "That all you have? No, no, this is a good start. They rent any other space from you?"

He listened for a minute. "No, that's OK. Appreciate your help. If we need anything more, I'll get back to you." He hung up the phone, and I looked over at what he'd written. A corporate name, a phone number and an address.

"Is that…" I asked.

"Looks like it." It was the address where Ricardo was living, the house owned by Nilady Cruz. "It doesn't tell us anything much, but it's another piece of the puzzle."

I didn't want to wait for Vito, so after Roly left, I did some searching on Nilady Cruz myself. I found a Cuban exile's Spanish-language website that she'd been interviewed on. The automatic translation into English wasn't great, but I discovered that she had been a doctor in Havana until her brother was arrested for anti-communist activities. His scandal tarred her, too, and she left for Mexico, where she became a chemistry professor at a university in Monterrey.

She had come to the US a year before, but that was

all I was able to find. I was drumming my fingers on my desk again, impatient to know more, when Roly buzzed me. "Come on down to Vito's office and let's talk about what you guys discovered last night."

Vito was behind his desk, Roly sitting across from him along with a blonde female agent named Christine Potts. "You know Chris, from the Health Care Fraud Task Force?" Roly asked.

"Just to say hello to." We shook hands. Since all the available chairs were taken, I leaned against the door.

"Chris has been investigating pill mills." He turned to her. "You want to tell us what you've found?"

"I'm sure you've heard of the operations that dispense oxycodone and other semi-synthetic opioids," she said. "It used to be that ninety of the top hundred doctors prescribing oxycodone were in Florida, most of them here in Broward County. We thought we'd knocked them out, but it looks like we've got a new operation going. Run by Nilady Cruz."

13

NERDS WITH GUNS

Vito swiveled his monitor around so that all of us could look at the photos on screen. Nilady Cruz was a tall woman with coffee-colored skin and black hair pulled back from her forehead. She wore funky rectangular glasses and had a distinctive mole on her right cheek.

"The operation is very clandestine," Chris Potts continued. "Every time we find an address on one of these pill mills, the group behind them is one step ahead of us, and the place is closed down by the time we get there. There's no signage, and the word passes from addict to addict. We're having a hard time getting a handle on her operation, but from what we can tell, she's not just writing prescriptions, but filling them right there."

"One-stop shopping," Vito said.

Chris nodded. "She doesn't accept credit cards or personal checks. Strictly cash only. Addicts have been driving in from as far as West Virginia."

"Has Ricardo Lopez's name ever come up in your investigations?" I asked. "Is he a friend of hers? A relative? Somebody who works for her?"

"Haven't come across him yet," Chris said. "But if you guys are nosing around Dr. Cruz, you've got to do it without jeopardizing my case."

"We discovered a house in Miramar registered in her name," I said.

Chris nodded. "Already know about that. But we don't have enough concrete information yet to get a search warrant for the premises or an arrest warrant for Cruz."

"Thanks, Chris," Roly said. "We're going to do some brainstorming and we'll get back to you."

She stood up and walked out, and I slid into her chair. It was uncomfortably warm, but I sucked it up.

"This is Cruz's résumé," Vito said, passing a piece of paper toward me. It showed that she had a degree in medicine from the University of Santiago de Cuba. She had been a practicing doctor at the Hospital Ciro Garcia in Havana until 2002, when she was released from her duties there.

There was no record of her until 2005, when she emigrated to Mexico and became a professor of chemistry at the Universidad Autónoma de Nuevo León in Monterrey. She stayed there until she came to the US in 2009.

"I did some searching myself," I said. I told them about the blog and her brother's activities, and they both nodded.

"Any idea how she's connected to Lopez?" Vito asked.

I ran through what I knew of Ricardo Lopez, which wasn't much. "We can run his prints," I said. "See what comes up. Maybe he has a police record that will connect him to her."

"Need something with his prints on it," Vito said.

I jumped up. "Be right back."

I hurried down the hall, sideswiping the SAC in my hurry. "I like to see my agents moving fast," he said. "But be careful, too."

"Sorry!"

I grabbed the grocery bag holding the pool cue and returned to Vito's office. "The cue Ricardo was using last night," I said.

Vito nodded. "Good thinking. Take it over to the evidence lab and see if they can lift any prints, then run them through IAFIS. It's your case, rookie," he said. "Go see what you can figure out and then let us know."

I carried the grocery bag gingerly around the maze of offices until I reached the lab, where I talked with a Chinese-American agent with the unlikely name of Wagon.

He was wearing a white lab coat, with a pair of goggles hanging around his neck. "You think you could see if there are any prints on this?" I asked him.

"I can try."

I pulled up a barstool to watch as Wagon dusted the pool cue, starting from the handle. "I'm using a combination of aluminum powder and volcanic dust," he said as he worked. "You know much about prints?"

"Only what they taught at Quantico," I said.

"Take a look up there for a refresher." He pointed to a poster on the wall that showed arches, whorls, and loops. Loops were the most common pattern, with approximately 60 percent of fingers showing them. 30 percent had whorls, and only about 5 to 10 percent showed arches. It was rare to have more than one pattern on any given finger, but a person's hand could contain different patterns on each finger.

Wagon brushed the excess powder off the cue, and I leaned over to watch. Most of the aluminum was smudged, but Wagon pointed to an arched pattern appearing a couple of inches up on the handle. "You might be getting lucky," he said, "That looks like a pretty good specimen."

He fed the print into the system. "This could take anywhere from twenty minutes to two hours to get a match, if he's ever been printed before," he said. "I'll e-mail you when something comes in."

I went back to Roly's office, where he and Vito were still talking. "I'd like to go back out to that warehouse where Ricardo Lopez went this morning," I said. "I'm not going to follow him or engage anybody. I just want to see what's going on there and if there's a connection to the big jewelry show at the convention center."

Vito looked at Roly, who nodded. "Just be careful," Roly said. "Remember the fruit of the poisoned tree."

"I know." I recited the rule by heart. "Any evidence obtained from an illegal arrest, unreasonable search, or coercive interrogation must be excluded from trial." I looked at them. "I did graduate from the academy, you know."

"But you're still a rookie," Vito said. "And it's our job to make sure you don't screw up." He waved his hand at me. "Now go."

I went.

Ricardo's SUV was parked in front of the warehouse, a busy complex, cars and trucks coming and going. Each bay was laid out the same way, at least from the outside. A metal door that rolled up, big enough to drive through. A smaller door to the right, which probably led into an office.

I circled around and parked in front of the Jamaican restaurant across the street. A gentle reggae beat streamed out of speakers above the door, along with the mixed scent of meat patties and marijuana. I turned off the engine, opened the windows, and leaned back. One of the items we had been instructed to purchase during our training at the FBI academy was a good pair of binoculars; I kept mine in my glove compartment. I pulled them out and focused on the warehouse.

A light breeze stirred the palm trees on the grassy strip between the parking lot and the street, which made it tolerable to sit without air conditioning. Cars came and went around me, and groups of high school kids passed on the sidewalk, talking and laughing and pushing each other.

While I waited I tried to make sense of everything I'd learned. But no matter how I shifted the puzzle pieces around, I couldn't figure out why Ricardo would have been interested in a diagram of the Miami Beach Convention Center. Had he asked Paco for it on behalf of Nilady Cruz? But what would a chemist running a pill mill want with gemstones?

Around two o'clock, a delivery truck pulled up and a hunky guy in brown shirt and shorts opened the back door and began pulling out a series of boxes stamped "TEKSTIIL" in big letters and putting them on his dolly.

I took a bunch of photos, because it seemed stupid not to.

The driver pressed a buzzer on the wall next to the office door. Ricardo stepped out, and the driver handed him an electronic device to sign, and then followed Ricardo inside, towing the dolly. I used my phone to google the word on the box and discovered it was the name of a textile company in Estonia.

I pulled up pictures of quaint embroidered skirts, slippers, and mittens. What was Ricardo Lopez doing importing that kind of stuff? Was I wrong about his involvement in criminal activities? Maybe he was just a working stiff at a warehouse.

Then the hunky delivery guy came back out, and I was momentarily distracted as I watched him climb back into his truck and drive away. I must have accidentally touched something on my phone, because a screen popped up with an article about drug abuse in Estonia.

The drug of choice for injectors in most EU countries was heroin, but in Estonia it was 3-methylfentanyl, or, as it was called there, White Persian. 3-methylfentanyl had first emerged back in the 1980s, and was popular because regular opiate screenings couldn't detect its presence in urine. It was one of the most potent drugs widely sold on the black market, and could be anywhere from four hundred to six thousand times more powerful than morphine.

One gram of the pure stuff could be diluted down to produce several thousand dosage units. That made it easy to bring in a lot of cash from a fairly small shipment.

Maybe Chris Potts was wrong, and the pain clinic wasn't dispensing oxycodone at all, but White Persian, imported from Estonia and then diluted by Nilady Cruz, an experienced chemist.

I was excited. I might have cracked the whole case open, or discovered a new angle on drug smuggling. But then I took a deep breath. All I had was a hunch, and even though

I was just a rookie, I knew I needed a lot more proof before I could take my hunch anywhere.

I drove back to the office, where I found an e-mail from Wagon saying that he'd found a fingerprint match. Ricardo Lopez, Mexican national with a green card obtained two years before. One misdemeanor for indecent exposure last year in Wilton Manors.

There was no indication of how he'd obtained that green card. They weren't easy to get, and wondered if his really belonged to him or, like Paco's Social Security number, was one he shared with other illegals. I printed out the e-mail and a couple of the pictures from my phone, and walked down the hall to Roly's office.

I showed him the fingerprint report. "Good job picking up that pool cue," he said. "How'd you manage to get it while you were following him?"

"I had a friend who works at the bar grab it for me," I said.

Roly sat back in his chair and looked at me. There was no way he could know what my relationship was with Lester. And why should it matter?

"You have something a lot of agents lack, Angus," he said. "You have this ability to talk to people, to make friends, to gather information. That's the kind of thing they can't teach you at Quantico. You're going to make a terrific agent one day."

I was surprised by the praise, but I mumbled a thank you. "There's something more." I showed him the photos I'd printed, and he peered down at them.

"What am I looking at?"

"While I was watching the warehouse where Ricardo

Lopez works, a delivery arrived. I looked up the logo on the boxes, and they came from a company in Estonia." I leaned forward. "You know about 3-methylfentanyl, aka White Persian?"

"Heard the name. What is it?"

I explained about its potency, and how easy it was to dilute it. "I think Nilady Cruz is buying this White Persian in Estonia and smuggling it into the US in shipments of these Estonian textiles."

Roly steepled his fingers. "That's a pretty big leap."

"I know. Which is why I came to you. Let's say it's a hypothesis. How can we prove it?"

"We don't have to. We take the information to Chris Potts and see what she can do with it."

We found Chris in her office, a larger one than either Roly's or Vito's, with a window that looked out toward the I-75 highway, just beyond our property. One wall was filled with books, while huge file cabinets occupied the other two walls.

"It's your hypothesis, Angus," Roly said, as we sat down. "You play it out."

My heart thumped as I explained my surveillance and my conclusions. "Nilady Cruz was a professor of chemistry in Mexico," I said. "She has the ability to thin out the raw material."

I sat back while she thought. I doubted Chris would laugh at me, but patronizing me would be just as bad.

Instead, she nodded. "It makes sense. We've been quizzing our confidential informants about oxycodone, and nobody has anything to report. But there's something being sold out of those pain clinics, and it could well be White

Persian, or some custom variation Nilady Cruz has come up with. Good job, Angus. I'll take it from here."

Despite the praise I'd received from Roly and Chris, I was discouraged as I walked back to my office. It looked like I was being shuttled back to my desk, and maybe I belonged there, like Wagon. I was an accountant, after all— just another nerd with a gun.

14

MARDI GRAS BEADS

By the time I reached my desk, I was in full pity-party mode. I slid back into my chair and stared at the screen. But when my computer came back to life, with the FBI logo on the log-in screen, I sat up. I was a special agent with the Federal Bureau of Investigation. I had my own case—the potential theft at the jewelry show. And it was up to me to figure out what was going on.

It was Thursday afternoon, and the jewelry show was set to open in a week. On a hunch, I checked to see if there were any jewelry dealers from Estonia coming to the show. Maybe more of the raw material was coming in with precious gems?

No luck. The only kind of gem Estonia was known for was amber, and there were no dealers who specialized in fossilized tree resin. There were no vendors coming from Estonia or from bordering countries. I even checked for any from Finland because it was a short boat trip away, across the Gulf of Finland. No luck.

Was it possible that Nilady Cruz and her drug operation were not connected to the jewelry show at all? That Ricardo was operating on his own? Given what I knew of him, it seemed unlikely, but he was the link that connected the jewelry show and the pill mill investigation.

Paco's call to the tip line had kicked off this whole investigation, and within hours of that he'd gotten into Ricardo's SUV, only to end up dead in a canal. So even if the two cases weren't connected, I needed to know more about Ricardo.

I thought back to the metaphor Vito had used, about information needing to be like milk—it was only useful if it was fresh. I doubted that they served milk at the bar at Equinox, but I was pretty certain I could find some information there about Ricardo—if I talked to the right people.

I stopped at Whole Foods on my way home, ladled out a large container of butternut squash soup, and made myself a big salad at the bar. When I got home, Jonas wasn't there, but I could tell from the discarded tie and dress shirt on the sofa that he'd passed through on his way out somewhere. I ate my soup and salad in front of *Jeopardy!*, matching questions to answers along with the contestants. I guess even when I don't know for sure, so I would have lost anything I won on one of the daily doubles. Have to stick with Uncle Sam, then.

I kept hoping Jonas would come back to go to Equinox with me, but no luck. Around ten I put on a pair of skinny jeans and deck shoes and a T-shirt that read "I can't even think straight," which hung loose enough to cover my gun in its thumb holster.

Lester wasn't on the door; the bouncer was a black guy, nowhere near as bulked up as Lester, or as cute. That was a relief; it meant that I could focus on my case without any distractions. And that was important. I was determined to prove I deserved the responsibility that had been handed to me.

I ordered a beer and walked over to the pool tables, where I recognized the older guy, intent on his shot, as the one who'd been playing with Ricardo the night before. "Anybody got winners?" I asked his opponent, a skinny Latin guy I thought I recognized from that photo on the wall of Lazy Dick's.

"You 'ave money, you can play," he said, with a pretty heavy Spanish accent.

I stacked my quarters on the edge of the table and leaned back to watch the game. The skinny guy's name was Enrique and the older guy was Peter. Enrique was a lot better than Peter, and within about ten minutes he was aiming at the eight ball. "Corner pocket," he said, and leaned down to sight his shot.

I realized why Peter had lost; he was a lot more interested in watching Enrique's ass than in playing pool. "You wan' to play?" Enrique asked, standing back up after landing the eight ball just where he had promised.

"Cool." I slipped my quarters in the slot and racked the balls. "Did I see you here last night?" I asked Peter. "Playing with Ricardo Lopez?"

I leaned down to sight a shot while I waited for his response.

"Maybe. You know Ricardo?"

"Mutual friends. He fooled around with my roommate." I slammed the cue into the pile of balls, and the red three went into the side pocket. "I've got solids."

"Who's your roommate?" Peter asked.

I moved around the table, looking for the best shot. "Jonas Sackler. You know him?"

Peter shook his head, but Enrique laughed and said, "Sad Sack? I know heem."

I looked over at him and chuckled. "That's harsh, dude." I sighted my ball and said, "Number two, front left."

I hit the ball, and it went just where I wanted, with a satisfying clunk. "Jonas was looking for him the other day, but Ricardo never called."

"He don't do that kind of thing no more," Enrique said.

"You mean hustling?" I twisted to the right, sighting the number one ball. I didn't think I could make the shot, but it was the best I could try. I announced, shot, and watched the cue ball carom off the number one in the wrong direction.

"He never hustle," Enrique said, picking up his cue. "Jus' pick up little cash sometimes." He sighted the number twelve and called the side pocket. He made that shot, and then the next two. Then he didn't nudge the number seven hard enough, and it stopped short of the pocket.

"Why you look for him?"

"Feel bad for Jonas," I said, leaning over the table, looking for a good shot. "Thought maybe I could hook him up. You know how I can reach Ricardo?"

"Don't waste your time," Peter said. "Ricardo says he's got a gig going on, gonna put him good for money for long time."

"Anything to do with jewelry?" I asked.

Peter looked at me. "You mean like rings and necklaces and shit? He wears a pretty nice gold bracelet but that's the only jewelry I know about with him. Though he said he moved in with his cousin's girlfriend, so he don't gotta pay rent no more. Maybe he's buying himself a diamond cock ring with all the money he's saving." He leered at me.

So Nilady Cruz wasn't his cousin, but his cousin's girlfriend. I was so busy making connections I messed up the next shot. When Enrique got control of the table, he took out the rest of the stripes. Peter had already put his quarters down for the next game.

"You talk to Ricardo, you tell him Jonas wants to see him," I said to Enrique.

He shrugged. "If I see him."

I looked around the bar. It appeared to be Lester's night off, and I had the information I'd come for, so I was going to be a good boy and go home to sleep. On my way, I called Danny's cell, but he didn't answer. "It's me, bro," I said. "Call me when you need to talk."

Friday morning I woke early and spent an hour working out. Showering at the gym is always fun, exchanging covert glances with the other naked guys. But my mind was on business. I changed into my work clothes: khaki slacks, white oxford cloth button down shirt and navy blazer, with a Penn State tie in navy blue patterned with white lion's heads. I didn't have the accumulation of suits that the long-time agents had and I wasn't eager to drop every spare penny into my wardrobe.

Within a few minutes of getting into the office, I was called into a meeting in the big conference room, which had been set up classroom-style with rows of chairs facing a screen and a tall rack of electronic equipment. The projector was on, showing someone's desktop, but I couldn't tell whose it was.

Roly and Vito were there, as well as a bunch of other agents I knew. The SAC stood at the podium talking with Chris Potts, and within a moment or two Chris had called us to attention. "Thanks to some diligent observation by Agent Green, we've identified a warehouse we believe is holding a significant quantity of raw 3-methylfentanyl prior to manufacturing and distribution."

My adrenaline level jumped. My information had been useful. How cool was that?

Chris walked the team through the basics of White Persian. "Overnight we got confirmation from the legat in Tallinn that this company, Textiil, is connected to a drug manufacturing operation there."

The FBI had legal attachés, or legats, in various countries around the world. And from all that time spent poring over maps with my dad, I knew that Tallinn was the capital of Estonia. Thanks, Dad.

"On the basis of that information, we're getting a search warrant approved." She turned to the SAC. "Sir?"

He stepped up to the podium. "We need to take maximum precautions here, because if this is a drug smuggling operation, those inside the warehouse could be heavily armed. All available personnel are needed for an immediate raid."

He looked down at the podium and began reading names, giving us our assignments. There were six guys on the SWAT team; they were going in first. I was assigned to bring a laptop with me to inventory whatever was in the warehouse, along with Zolin, a moon-faced Mexican-American from Arizona.

Zolin was a couple of years older than I was. He'd graduated from law school but hated practicing, and had joined the Bureau the year before. When I first arrived in Miami I had hoped to befriend him, as the other junior agent in the office, but he had a wife and a baby. His last name began with an X and no one besides him could pronounce it, so he was usually Agent X, which was kind of cool.

The SAC looked back up. "Gear up and get ready to roll out."

I ditched my jacket and tie, replacing them with my Kevlar vest and FBI windbreaker, and grabbed my Bureau-issued laptop. Out in the parking lot, I joined a group of agents getting into an SUV. It was a gray day, a solid mass of cloud cover overhead, humidity in the high double digits. A skein of geese flew over the field office and a pair of great blue herons picked at tiny fish in one of the retention ponds.

Everyone was talking and joking, but the adrenaline level was high. It was the first major raid I'd taken part in, and though it was my information that had led to it happening, I was determined to keep my mouth shut, pay attention, and stay out of trouble.

We drove north on I-75, threading our way through heavy traffic. Two motorcycle cops led a funeral cortege in front of us, constantly circling back and forth from front to rear to make sure the line remained intact, and my heart thumped so loud I was afraid the agents beside me would hear it.

A couple of squad cars from the Broward Sheriff's

Office blocked the access route to the warehouse complex, their overhead lights flashing. I figured we had to be in an unincorporated part of Broward County—one that the BSO patrolled. I didn't see Ricardo's SUV in the parking lot.

Our vehicle curled past the deputies and pulled up at the rear of the warehouse complex, where it backed up against a canal. A few cars were parked behind other bays, but nothing behind the one where I'd seen Ricardo the day before.

What if I was wrong? Or what if they'd already moved the boxes? Should I have stayed there the day before, called in my information, followed Ricardo as he left?

I took a deep breath. I was only one part of this operation, and I'd done my part.

As the deputies emptied people from the other warehouses and led them off to the side, the other agents and I spilled out. I kept my laptop in a pack on my back, so that my hands were free if I needed to use a radio or a weapon. I was hyped up from the buzz of activity around me.

"Warrant on the way," Chris Potts said through our radios. "ETA ten minutes."

When I was a kid, Danny and I fished along the banks of the Lackawanna River, which ran through Scranton, and since moving to South Florida I was often drawn to the ever-present water around me, from ocean to river to lakes. While I waited for the warrant to arrive, I walked back toward the canal to watch the water.

I followed the eddies of the current around a half-submerged log until it pushed up against a blue bicycle half in the water along the canal bank. The bike had been smashed, as if it had been run over by a truck, but the purple Mardi Gras beads wrapped around the handlebars were still intact.

15

EVIDENCE RECOVERY

My radio crackled to life before I could find either Roly or Vito to tell them about the bicycle. The SWAT team was about to take the warehouse.

An agent in full gear walked up to the door and rapped on the metal, announcing, "FBI!" Three other agents stood poised with Remington 12-gauge shotguns with fourteen-inch barrels and Heckler & Koch 10-mm-barrel guns that could work in automatic or semi-automatic mode. I had trained with both weapons, as well as with the .40-caliber Glock 22 that was our standard service weapon, but I was by no means the kind of expert marksman that the SWAT guys were.

Vito came up behind me and clapped me on the shoulder, startling me. "Your first big op?" he asked.

"Yeah."

"You piss your pants yet?"

I scowled at him. "I'm okay."

He laughed. "Don't worry if you get nervous, rookie. Happens to all of us. You know what I do?"

I shook my head.

"I always say to myself, 'It's the next one that kills you,'" he said. "Not this op, but the next one. That's how I make it through."

I hadn't been thinking about getting killed at all until then. The agent at the door banged once more, and still got no answer. "Out back," I began. "By the canal...."

Vito stepped away from me before I could finish. The agent by the door stepped aside, and another guy with a rammer walked up. The rammer was about forty pounds, basically a concrete tube with handles. The agent holding it smashed the door handle, destroying the lock and sending the door swinging open. Then he stepped aside as the rest of the team streamed in.

It didn't look like there was anyone inside, and a moment later the all clear came over the radio. The SWAT team left to take up defensive positions outside the warehouse in case someone showed up, and the evidence recovery team went in next, before the rest of us contaminated the scene. One of them raised the big metal door so we could see in. It was a tall, echoing space, and I saw the boxes from Estonia stacked along one wall.

I was relieved. The boxes were still there.

But what if I'd been wrong, and this was just a shipment of clothes and linens?

I spotted Roly and walked over to him to tell him about the bicycle, but he had something else in mind. He pointed to one of the ERT team members, a skinny Latin guy with greased-down hair. He had a hefty SLR camera with a big lens, and it looked like he was taking wide-angle shots of the warehouse complex.

"Here's a refresher for you," Roly said to me. "Why isn't he using a video camera?"

"The FBI never takes video footage of a scene," I said, remembering what I had learned at the academy.

"Why not?"

"You never know what might get into the video that might turn out to be prejudicial to a case down the road," I said. "Like, an agent joking in the background could show evidence of prejudice."

"And?"

"Video gives you too much information," I said. "It makes it hard to focus on what's important. Taking still pictures makes you pay attention to what you want in the shot. You have to make conscious decisions about angles and lighting and what to include or leave out."

"Very good." We watched as the photographer turned his camera on the crowd that had assembled to watch us work. I'd heard that it was true that criminals often returned to see first-hand the destruction they had wrought. And whoever rented the warehouse might have come over to see what was going on. So shots of the crowd might prove useful in the future.

"I've got to talk to you," I said to Roly. "About Paco."

His cell rang, and he pulled it out of his pocket. "Gotta take this. I'll catch you later."

He moved away, and I watched the ERTs work, taking photographs of the warehouse and the contents, dusting for fingerprints and so on. It was hot out there, and I stripped off my windbreaker and my bulletproof vest, leaning them on the ground with the backpack containing my laptop. I kept one eye on the bicycle; I didn't want anyone to touch it, but I wasn't going to make it a big deal unless I had to.

The ERT members went in and out of the bay in a controlled pattern, making sure to disturb as little of the materials as possible. It was Locard's principle in action: everywhere you go, you leave part of yourself behind, and take away part of the place itself. By restricting themselves to one path in and out, they minimized the effects of their actions.

I watched as the photographer moved in closer to the bay itself. Another agent, a blonde woman, recorded a paper list of everything that was photographed, including the specifics of each exposure. It was all part of building a case for prosecution.

A third agent had a pad and pencil and was drawing sketches of the property. With a drawing you could remove unnecessary detail that crowded a photo, and the act of drawing helped the eye focus on what was important.

It took the ERTs the better part of an hour to collect everything from the inside. At one point I saw a couple of them down on the concrete floor, examining some kind of stain. Once they finished inside, I was summoned. I took a last look at the bicycle as I pulled my laptop out of my backpack.

As I settled down beside Zolin, Chris Potts opened the first box with a wicked-looking knife and held up what looked like a little girl's dress in a vibrant orange color. It had an elaborately embroidered yoke in a pattern of dots and lines. She used her knife to cut through the seam, and a small packet of white powder fell out.

There was a notable hush in the room. I leaned over and whispered to Zolin, "Do you know what 3-methylfentanyl looks like?"

He shook his head. "They'll have to take it to the lab for testing."

It was slow, tedious work, listing every marking on every box, then inventorying all the materials inside. Mittens, scarves, sweaters, dresses, each one photographed, measured, described, and examined to see if it contained contraband.

I kept looking at the stain on the concrete floor. Was it blood? Had someone been killed there?

It took us nearly three hours to inventory everything in the warehouse. As we finished with a box, one of Chris's agents loaded it into the back of an SUV for transport to the lab. My back ached from hunching over the laptop for so long without a break, and I was relieved when we finished the last box.

I stood up and flexed my back muscles. By then, most of the agents were gone, including the evidence recovery team. I saw Roly about to walk out. I yelled out, "Hey, Roly, I need to talk to you!"

He stopped and looked around, and I waved. He laughed about something with one of the other agents, then walked over to me.

"There's a bicycle out back," I said. "I saw it when we first got here. I think maybe it belonged to Paco."

"Show me." As we walked outside, he said, "Why didn't you talk to me as soon as you recognized the bicycle? Christ, Angus, we've been here all day."

I started to argue but stopped short. I wasn't going to

make any excuses. I should have focused on my own case, set my own priorities. "It won't happen again."

"Tell me the whole story, from the start."

I narrated as we walked around the building. When we got to the place where the bicycle lay against the berm, I pointed to it. "The purple Mardi Gras beads," I said. "See? It matches the description of the bike that the old guy said Paco used. Can we dust it for fingerprints, see if maybe it's his?"

He radioed for one of the evidence techs to come back. "Looks abandoned, doesn't it?" he asked me as we waited.

"Sure. But why does that matter?"

"Then we don't have to worry about curtilage, or the terms of the search warrant."

I nodded, remembering what I had learned about search warrants at the academy. They were very specific, directing us to search for certain items in certain places, for a specified period of time. I was pretty sure the one we had for the warehouse didn't include smashed-up bicycles far from the bay we had the warrant for.

But the fact that the bicycle had been wrecked, and was assumed to be trash, removed it from what was called the curtilage, the area immediately around the warehouse that could be reasonably assumed to be part of the premises itself.

Leave a bag of trash in the can right next to your house? We won't be able to look through it, because it's part of the curtilage. But take that same bag of trash out to the street, and you've given up your expectation that it remains your private property. The same was true of the broken-down bicycle.

A couple of large dark birds soared overhead in lazy

circles. "See those?" Roly said, pointing at the sky. "Turkey vultures. They're snowbirds—come down here from October to March looking for dead bodies to feed on."

I shuddered. "Human ones?"

"I doubt they discriminate. You ever go to the courthouse in downtown Miami, you'll see a whole flock of them roosting up on the roof." He leaned in close to me. "People say they're the ghosts of dead attorneys still hoping to win their cases." Then he laughed. "Come on, Angus, smile. You gotta joke around now and then, or this job gets to you."

I smiled, though I still found the vultures overhead creepy.

An evidence tech searched the area around the bike, then took fingerprints from it. Finally, he wrapped it in brown kraft paper from a huge roll, then loaded it in the back of a van. "There's a guy at the morgue called Paco Gonzalez," Roly said to him. "See if you can match any prints on the bike to him."

"That stain on the warehouse floor," I said to the tech. "Was that blood?"

"Looks like it."

"Can you see if it matches Paco?"

"That'll take time," the tech said. "But I'll put it on the list."

He left, and I stood there beside Roly, looking out at the canal. "I've got an idea," I said. I opened up the laptop again and plugged in the air card, allowing me to get Wi-Fi through a cell phone line.

"What are you doing?" Roly asked.

"Just a hunch." I pulled up Google Maps and typed in

the warehouse address. Then I zoomed out and pointed at my screen. "See this thin blue line? That's the canal in front of us. It runs all the way down to where Paco's body was found."

I remembered watching the current when I first walked down to the canal. I picked up a piece of coconut husk from the berm and tossed it into the canal, and watched as it landed, then began to float west toward the Everglades. "There's just a little current. His body could have floated down the canal to where it was found. The ME said he had been in the water for a while, and banged up against stuff as he moved."

"Good point," Roly said. He had brought his own car to the site, and we walked toward it. "You have any ideas on how these cases are tied together?"

"Only through Ricardo Lopez," I said. "He lives in the same house as Nilady Cruz, and he accepted the delivery of boxes yesterday, addressed to her company. As far as I know now, he was the last person to see Paco alive."

I took a breath. "What if Ricardo found out about Paco's meeting with you, and he picked up Paco on Saturday afternoon and brought him out here. He was killed here, and his body dumped in the canal."

"The bicycle?"

"Maybe Ricardo offered Paco a ride to work," I said. "Paco wouldn't have accepted the ride if he didn't have a way to get home. So Ricardo had to take the bicycle too. But he didn't need to keep it once Paco was dead."

"You have any leads on Ricardo?" Roly asked.

"Only his cell phone number. I had my roommate call him, but Ricardo never called him back."

"Your roommate?"

"Jonas hangs out at Lazy Dick's. He had a one-night stand with Ricardo a couple of months ago. I asked him to make a booty call but Ricardo never called back."

As soon as the words were out of my mouth, I worried what Roly would say. Something derogatory about gay men having sex all the time?

"Young guys," Roly said, shaking his head. "I thank God for the day I met my wife so I didn't have to screw around anymore."

I was surprised and relieved.

"I'll see if I can get a trap and trace on the number," Roly continued. That was a court order to capture incoming and outgoing calls from a phone number.

"You have enough information to request one of those?" I asked.

He shrugged. "I can try. He was the last person seen with the victim. If we can place the victim here where the drugs were stored, there's a way to prove the connection."

"Should I notify the BSO detective about the blood on the floor of the warehouse?"

"Hold off on that. We don't know that it's blood, and we don't know that it belongs to Paco. Once we're sure, we'll pass the information on."

We stopped at a burger joint on the way back to the office and got takeout, and I ate a very late lunch at my desk, in between e-mailing the spreadsheet I'd put together at the warehouse to Zolin, who would combine them, and writing up my notes on the FD302. By the end of the day, I was exhausted but also thrilled. I'd survived my first big operation.

Then I remembered what Vito had said while we waited outside the warehouse. Would the next one kill me?

16
LIKE A STRAIGHT GUY

That night I was happy to be able to go home and relax, without any pressure to go out. I texted a little with Lester and made plans to get together over the weekend, and watched the beginning of a movie with Jonas, but I couldn't keep my eyes open.

Friday morning I heard that the test results had come back on the packages sewn into the Estonian textiles. They had tested positive for 3-methylfentanyl. There was still no indication of where Nilady's lab was, or any address where her pill clinics could be found.

I focused on my own case. I wanted to know everything about the jewelry show and the convention center. I spent hours looking at information about jewelry shows around the country, about security for them, about robberies and attempted robberies at shows.

Dealers had been followed hundreds of miles after a trade show in Chicago to be robbed at a highway rest stop.

Ethnic Chinese employees of a California jewelry company had been accosted in their hotel room in Manhattan by men speaking Mandarin and English. Another pair of dealers attending an arts and crafts show had been robbed at gunpoint outside their North Jersey hotel.

Those were outliers, though. The shows seemed to have sufficient security, and the dealers were savvy enough to take precautions. What kind of vulnerability had Ricardo discovered in the plan Paco had provided him that would enable him to succeed?

I went back to Vito's milk metaphor. I needed to get out and collect more intelligence on Ricardo and hope that some small detail led me to the right conclusions.

Late in the afternoon, I told Roly what I wanted to do. "Just remember to keep your focus on this convention center thing. That's your case."

"And I might find out more about Nilady Cruz while I'm investigating."

He shook his head. "Don't go there. If you do hear something, you pass it on. You don't act on it. You don't want to stick your nose into the drug case because you'll just crap it up."

"Thanks for your faith in me."

"It's nothing to do with you personally, Angus. I can see you're a smart guy, that you're dedicated. But you have to remember the rules."

"I understand."

"Call me or Vito if you run into any trouble." He stood up. "You're doing great, Angus. Most agents on their first case can barely find their dicks with two hands. You've turned up some good information already."

I drove home feeling excited. Roly thought I was doing a good job. That meant a lot.

Jonas wasn't home when I got there. I got another of the Sea Dog Raspberry Wheat beers from the fridge and sat back on my bed, trying to relax. I was about halfway through the beer, no closer to relaxation, when Danny called.

"Hey, bro," I said. "How's it going?"

"I've been watching the other servers, like you told me to," he said. "Boy, you never know what's going on around you until you start to pay attention."

"What did you find?"

"Angie's boyfriend comes in every night for a beer and a calzone, and she never rings him up. Louie the busboy breaks at least two glasses every night. And my buddy Rocket, who works the same shift I do, has a serious coke habit I never knew about."

"But did you see anybody using a machine to scan credit cards?"

"No. But I'm keeping my eye out, Angus. I totally am."

"That's great, Danny. Maybe I'll make you into an FBI agent one day."

"No way," he said, but I could hear the pride in his voice.

"Just be careful, bro. Don't do anything dumb and stay away from the guy with the coke. Remember, you're working there for a purpose—you're going to Italy, just like Dad would have wanted."

Danny was only five when our dad died, so he didn't remember the way Dad had longed to see the world. My dad was good with numbers, just like me. He'd been going to college for an accounting degree when he met my mom. But after they got married, he dropped out and got himself a bookkeeping job for a coal mining company in Scranton. It wasn't until I was a teenager and taking a sex ed class that I realized my parents had only been married seven months when I was born.

My dad's dreams were a big reason why I joined the FBI. When I was a kid, he'd sit with me on his lap and the atlas open, and his fingers would trace all these places with exotic names—Timbuktu, the Seychelles, Gabon, Tahiti. "I was gonna go these places, Angus," he'd say. "Maybe I still will. Someday, when you and your brother are grown up."

He'd never lived to see us grown, though. He had a heart attack at work one day; keeled over at his desk preparing payroll records for the miners. My mom wouldn't even let me see him in his coffin.

I looked at the clock after I hung up with Danny. It was six thirty, and I'd have to hustle if I wanted to make it to Lazy Dick's before happy hour ended. Somebody at the bar had to have information on Ricardo Lopez, and I was the man to discover it.

I pulled on my skinny jeans again, this time matched with a plaid, short-sleeved shirt that I could leave untucked to camouflage my gun. I found the picture of the Labor Day fiesta I had taken off the wall at Lazy Dick's, folded it, and stuck it in my shirt pocket.

Jonas came in as I was about to leave, and I told him my plans. "You sure you want to do this, Angus?" he asked. "Dude, if Ricardo's really mixed up in some trouble, I'd steer away from him if I were you."

"It's my job, dude," I said. "You don't have to come along if you don't want to."

He shook his head. "I never thought I'd turn down the chance to go bar crawling with you, but I'll stay right here."

"Suit yourself."

The half-priced margaritas at Lazy Dick's were watered down, so I ordered one and nursed it as I stood in a corner of the room and removed the photo from my shirt pocket.

Of the seven men in the picture, I recognized Paco, Ricardo, Enrique, Jonas, and the busboy I'd spoken to when I first began looking for Paco. When I caught sight of him clearing a table I walked over. "Hey, Usnavy, how's it going?"

He looked at me warily.

"I'm Angus. Remember me?" I lowered my voice and leaned my head in close. "I wanted to let you know I found out what happened to Paco."

"He dead, right?"

I nodded. "You knew? Or just guessed?"

He continued loading his plastic bin with dirty dishes and glasses. "Guessed."

"Last person seen with him was Ricardo," I said. "You know any reason Ricardo might have a beef with him?"

He didn't say anything, just shook his head.

"How about jewelry," I said. "Diamonds, fancy watches, that kind of thing. Ricardo ever talk about that?"

"He have one fancy gold bracelet," he said. "Always brag about guy who give it to him." He shook his head. "Married guy back in Mexico. No good ever come of that."

That was the second time someone had mentioned Ricardo's bracelet. I'd have to ask Jonas if he had noticed it.

Usnavy picked up his bin, ready to return to the kitchen. "Know anything at all that might help me?" I asked.

"He used to be nice guy," Usnavy said. "Ricardo. Then

that cousin of his, she come and fill his head with all kinds of crap. She tell him he need to be himself, that if she can be with who she love, then so can he, if he make it happen. He move in with her, then he start to change, to be real jerk."

"His cousin? I thought he was living with his cousin's girlfriend."

He cocked his head like he didn't understand the problem. "*Lesbianas*. His cousin name Violeta, but she no flower." He bunched up his hands and squared his shoulders in a bodybuilder pose. "Tough *mujer*," he said. Then he grabbed the container of dirty dishes and hurried back to the kitchen.

Duh. I'd been thinking like a straight guy. Just because somebody had a girlfriend, I'd assumed that somebody was male.

17
BOUNCING LIKE TIGGER

I looked back at the picture. The other two men were older, in their fifties or sixties. Wilted Flowers, as Helen Wheels would call them. Men who had once been beautiful, and now struggled to maintain an illusion of youth with expensive face creams, endless gym workouts, and discreet plastic surgery.

One of the men in the picture stood beside the bar. About five foot eight, thinning dark hair precisely combed, wearing a Brooks Brothers polo shirt. He was talking to a young blond twink who kept scanning the room for someone, only occasionally nodding to the older man. I lingered in the corner, keeping my eye on them, until the twink finally broke away to go after a tattooed hunk in a muscle T-shirt, leaving the flower to wilt on the vine.

I walked up to him and stuck out my hand. "Hi, I'm Angus."

He looked at me and smiled. I could see he'd been quite good-looking when he was younger, and if my desire ran to daddies, he'd still be quite tasty. What a shame he was left hanging around this bar lusting after losers. "Tom," he said, and shook my hand.

His grip was firm. Up close I could see how close-shaven he was and get the faintest whiff of aftershave. Here was a guy who'd dressed up for the evening, not come by on his way home from work.

"It's not often that a handsome young man like you comes over to me," he said. "Especially one who's already got his own drink."

"I confess an ulterior motive." I reached into my pocket and extracted a business card—a bit difficult, given how tight my jeans were.

He looked around the bar and then surreptitiously pulled out a pair of reading glasses. He scanned the card and raised his eyebrows. "The FBI?"

"Do you remember when this picture was taken?" I asked, showing it to him.

He took the photo from me. "Ah, yes. Labor Day weekend. A good time was had by all. What's your interest in this happy event?"

"Not the event per se," I said. "But in this guy here." I pointed at Ricardo.

"Ricardo. I wondered when his activities might generate interest from law enforcement."

"You look like you're due for a refill, Tom," I said. "What do you say I buy you a drink and we retire to a quieter corner of the bar for a chat?"

"This evening gets more and more interesting," he said. "I'll have a vodka tonic."

I signaled to Kyle and nodded to Tom. Kyle quirked

an eyebrow at me. I sighed and nodded again. Yeah, I was buying.

While we waited, I turned back to Tom. "You live here in Wilton Manors?" I asked, catching myself just in time to not say Wilted Flowers.

"Not quite. A condo over on A1A."

Hmph. If Tom could afford to live by the beach, he didn't need me to buy him a drink. So much for my trying to act like a big shot. Kyle delivered Tom's drink, and I handed him a couple of bucks.

Tom led the way to a two-top in the back of the restaurant. "I'm going to get a lot of jealous looks," he said, as we settled down. "You have quite a reputation around here."

"You mean as an FBI agent?" I asked.

He guffawed. "You can't be that naïve, my young friend," He leaned forward. "You're gorgeous, and you have 'made for sex' stamped all over you."

I blushed, once again cursing my red hair and fair complexion. I struggled to remember that I was an FBI agent on a fact-finding mission. "Up at the bar you said you thought law enforcement might take an interest in Ricardo someday. Why?"

I assumed he was going to mention Ricardo's willingness to accept cash in exchange for sex, and I was surprised when he said, "All his drug connections, of course."

"Coke? Molly?" I asked.

Tom shook his head. "I was in a car accident a year ago," he said. "I was in a lot of pain, and my doctor was very hesitant to give me anything strong enough. Ricardo told me about a place where I could get what I needed."

"What kind of place?"

"A clinic he recommended." He used his fingers to make air quotes around the word clinic. "I tried to convince myself I was better than the other people there—the prostitutes and hillbillies and men and women so skinny you could tell their only appetite was for drugs. It took me a long time to realize that I was just like them."

He looked so sad that I wanted to hug him. But then he smiled. "It was hard, but I forced myself to scale back, little by little. I haven't taken anything stronger than an aspirin in six months."

"Good for you," I said. "What was it they were dispensing? Oxycodone?"

"I never knew the exact name of the stuff. They were red and white capsules that made all the pain go away."

"You have the name and address of this so-called clinic?"

"The place I went closed down about the time I cleaned myself up." He smiled. "Although the last time I saw Ricardo, he was kind enough to let me know the new address."

"Would you give it to me?"

He smiled, and I could almost see a double entendre floating out of his mouth. But instead he said, "I don't know that he ever gave me a street address," he said. "But he said it was on Oakland Park Boulevard just west of 441, between a karate dojo and a cell phone store."

"Thanks." I made a mental note of that. "Anything else you think I should know about Ricardo?"

"I assume you already know that he's available for sex for a price," Tom said. "Though I'm sure you've never paid for it in your life."

There was an undercurrent of bitterness there that I was sorry to hear. "I understood he wasn't quite that much of a mercenary," I said. "More like have sex, then ask for some cash as a handout."

Tom nodded. "That's the way I've heard it as well." There was a powerful gay grapevine where rumors circulated—bits of information like who might be interested in a certain activity, who should be avoided because of a particular condition, and so on. No one ever confessed to being the original source, and if confronted, the individual involved would always deny the allegation.

"I have a neighbor," Tom continued. "A very wealthy snowflake—you know, the type who only drops in during the winter for a few days at a time. He's done Ricardo a few favors in the past. One of those favors appears to be use of his townhouse on occasions when my neighbor isn't in residence."

I sipped my drink. "You ever discuss that with your neighbor?"

Tom smiled. "He and I aren't on the best of terms. Ricardo notwithstanding, my neighbor engages in some other practices I find unsavory."

I quirked an eyebrow, curious to know what Tom considered unsavory, but he didn't elaborate, and I didn't press. It wasn't relevant to my investigation, after all.

"Did Ricardo ever talk to you about jewelry?" I asked. "Jewelry dealers, wholesalers, trade shows, anything like that?"

"He had a friend back in Mexico who was in that business," Tom said, after a moment. "And when I say friend, you can see those quotation marks again."

"A trick?"

"More than that, I think. Ricardo was really carrying a

torch for him, but he was married, and you know how Latin cultures are when it comes to homosexuality."

I spent a few more minutes talking with Tom. He was an interesting guy, an attorney who had worked for a bank in Boston for a few decades, then taken an early retirement to enjoy the sun and scenery.

"You intrigue me, Angus," he said, as we were finishing up. "When I was your age, a gay man couldn't consider a career like yours. I'd love to talk more sometime."

"And I'd enjoy hearing more about your career choices, too. Do you have a card?"

I accepted it and said goodbye, and as soon as I got out to my car I wrote down the information on the pain clinic Ricardo had recommended. It was a lead I wanted to follow, but right then I needed to stay on course and learn as much as I could about Ricardo Lopez.

I drove to Equinox, where I ran into Jonas, and we hung out at the bar for a while as I scanned the room. Lester wasn't on duty, but the blond twink bartender was, and I asked him if Ricardo had been in that evening. "Haven't seen him, and I wouldn't expect him tonight," he said.

"Why not?"

"Look at the crowd."

I looked. The men were much more Anglo than the ones I'd seen on Wednesday night, and I realized why. There so many gay bars in Fort Lauderdale, and in order to differentiate themselves, they often ran special events—drag performers, '60s music, discounts for hotel and restaurant workers, and so on.

The theme at Equinox that night was ten-dollar buckets of beer. Not something that would attract Ricardo—but the next night was a Latin dance spectacular. I'd seen him move his hips, and if anything would draw him back there, that would be it.

I left Jonas at the bar and walked over to the pool tables. Neither of the guys who'd been playing with Ricardo on Wednesday night were there, and none of the men playing recognized his name. I cruised the room for a while but didn't recognize anyone.

When I got back to the bar, Jonas was moping into his beer. "I'm a loser and my life is a waste," he said.

"Give it a rest, Jonas," I said, sliding onto the stool next to him. "I'm not making any progress on my case, but you don't hear me whining."

"Fuck you, Angus."

"No thank you."

I thought for a second Jonas was going to throw his beer at me, but instead he laughed. "This place sucks."

"Yeah. But I'm going to have to come back tomorrow night. I figure it's more likely Ricardo will be here for the Latin dance thing. Will you come back with me?"

"Angus."

I hated the way he stretched my name out to multiple syllables. It reminded me of the way Danny would whine sometimes when he was a kid, and I already had one problem child little brother. But I needed a wingman. "Please?"

He crossed his arms over his chest. "I'm not letting you pimp me out."

I held up my hand. "I wouldn't dream of it. But I need your help, dude. Please?"

"All right. But you'll owe me."

I nodded. I had promised Roly and Vito that I'd use

everything at my disposal to find out why Paco had called that tip line, and why he had died. In that context, owing Jonas a favor was small beans.

Jonas and I drove home in our own cars and passed out in our own beds. Fortunately I'd had the presence of mind to take a couple of aspirins and drink a quart of water before I fell asleep, so when I woke up Saturday morning I had only a mild feeling of discomfort, a buzz at the back of my brain, and some queasiness in my stomach.

After an early-morning workout at the gym, I grabbed my digital camera and drove down to Oakland Park Boulevard, one of the main east-west thoroughfares through the central part of Broward County.

It was a hot, humid morning, the sun glinting off puddles of the rain that had fallen the night before, and traffic was heavy, big semi-trailers pumping air brakes as they came up on old folks who sat so low in the driver's seat it looked like there was no one there. Low-riders with booming bass that shook my car zigzagged around Canadian snowbirds.

I loved it all. South Florida was like a foreign country to me, after the coal mines and slag heaps of Scranton, and I wished my dad was still alive to come and visit me. He'd have relished hearing the island accents, the way cashiers switched flawlessly from Spanish to English as soon as I stepped up, the way a synagogue could be right next to an Apostolic church, the range of skin tones and hair colors.

I drove west, past jerk chicken restaurants and patio furniture stores, until I spotted the karate dojo and cell phone store I was looking for, in the middle of a nondescript strip shopping center. And between them, a glass door, the windows on either side covered in the kind of brown kraft paper the evidence tech had used to wrap Paco's bicycle. No sign, but an awful lot of people seemed to know what was inside.

I parked across the street and sat back in my car to watch. The center was a single story, with one row of parking spaces between it and the street. There was a constant stream of cars entering and exiting, and from my point of view it looked like a bumper car ride, as cars and trucks darted around each other, nearly backing into one another. Most of the moms delivering kids to the karate dojo couldn't park, just had to stop and drop. Several women going to the beauty salon parked in the lot next door and walked.

I focused on the clientele entering and exiting the unmarked door. Skinny bald men with arm-length tattoos, black men with dreadlocks, young women in baggy clothes, and unshaven older men streamed in and out of the doorway. Clouds moved in overhead for a brief sun shower, but that didn't stop anyone.

It couldn't be a real clinic. Every medical office I'd ever been to moved a lot more slowly than this place. There was barely enough time for a patient to enter the door, give a name, and then turn around and walk back out.

I pulled out my digital camera and began to snap photos of the clinic and the clientele. As I was zoomed in on the front door, a dark-skinned woman in a white doctor's coat stepped out. She looked vaguely familiar, and as I took a number of shots of her, I wondered where I'd seen her before.

I took some more photos, then figured I'd gotten enough. I pulled out and headed for home, but I kept thinking about the woman in the doctor's coat. I stopped in the parking lot of a post office and turned the camera on again to review the pictures of her.

Was it the white coat that had me confused? I zoomed in on her face. She wore funky glasses, the kind you'd see in an optometrist's ad. Was the spot on her cheek a beauty mark or a sign of skin cancer?

Focus, Angus.

It was the mole that clued me in. Could that be Nilady Cruz? I had to get to the office and check the pictures on my camera against the ones in the file.

I made a quick detour back home. I couldn't go into the office, even on a Saturday, in a pair of sweat pants and an old Penn State T-shirt.

I took a couple of minutes to e-mail the pictures to my FBI address, and once I was behind my desk I viewed the close-ups of the woman I thought was Nilady Cruz. It sure seemed like a match to me. I typed up an FD302 that began with the information Tom had given me about Ricardo's connection to the pain clinic, then recapped my surveillance that morning.

I finished the report and e-mailed it, along with the photos, to Chris Potts, and copied Vito and Roly on the e-mail. I hung around the office for another hour or two, reading about pill mills, and the more I read the more I was convinced that was the kind of operation going on behind those papered-over windows. Chris Potts had been looking for the location where Nilady Cruz was operating, and it was possible I'd found it.

I was bouncing around like Tigger, so excited, and I hated that it was Saturday and there was nobody to share my accomplishment with. Maybe I'd even get a commendation from the Special Agent in Charge. To Angus Green for exemplary investigative work.

Or maybe I was wrong, and I'd get yelled at for not focusing on my own case.

18

FLIRTATION

Jonas was gone when got home. I texted him to confirm our plans for Equinox that night and got no response, and a phone call went right to voice mail.

All afternoon, I kept checking my cell phone to make sure I hadn't missed a call—from Danny, Jonas, Chris Potts, Lester, anybody. I finally gave up and went for a jog around our neighborhood. When I got home it was seven o'clock, the sun was setting, and Jonas was just pulling up in the driveway.

"Where have you been?" I asked. "I've been waiting for you all day."

"Ease off, dude. I had a class."

"A class?"

"Yeah, I decided I need to get out of my shithole job, so I signed up for this advanced management certificate from FAU."

He told me all about the certificate, and the class, while

I bounced from foot to foot waiting to talk about that night. "Jesus, calm down, Angus," Jonas said. "You walk into Equinox like that, Ricardo's going to think you're a major squirrel and ignore you."

We walked into the house. "Chill," he said, pointing to the sofa. "I'll be back."

I took a couple of deep breaths and sat down, crossing my legs in the lotus position, with my hands resting on my knees and my palms open.

"Jesus, I don't know how you do that yoga stuff," Jonas said. He had a pouch of marijuana and a package of rolling papers in his hand.

"I can't smoke, Jonas," I said. "I'm a federal agent."

"You going to arrest me?" he asked, rolling the joint. "Come on, you know you want to get high with me. You need to relax."

"I'll have to count on legal means to relax," I said. "You go ahead, smoke. I'll get a beer at Equinox."

Maybe it was the yoga, or the secondhand high, or maybe I just felt better about my abilities because I'd successfully resisted temptation, but I calmed down. I drove us over to Equinox, and he pulled down the visor mirror. "How do I look?" he asked, as he smoothed his hair.

"Like a stud," I said. "How about me?"

I angled the rear view mirror and combed my hair. I hated the reddish-blond color, and my fair skin; it made me look like I was still a teenager.

"You always look good, Angus."

"And you know how to flatter a guy," I said.

We walked inside. There was no sign of Ricardo, so we went over to the bar, and I ordered us a couple of beers. We stood against the wall, talking and checking out the crowd. Lester wasn't at the door, though he'd be on duty at ten.

When he got in, I walked over to say hello. "Hey," he said.

"Hey." I wasn't sure if I was supposed to give him a kiss, or a hug; we'd slept together a couple of times but we weren't what I'd call a couple. And we were both working, when you got right down to it.

We settled for an awkward sort of hip bump. "I'm on until closing," he said. "Probably three o'clock. You going to be around that long?"

"Hard to say." I told him I was on the lookout for Ricardo.

"You be careful with him," Lester said.

"I will be."

We talked for a couple of minutes, then he turned to inspect some IDs, and I went back over to Jonas. "I hope we guessed right about Ricardo showing up for dance night."

As if on cue, Ricardo came through the door, accompanied by two other guys, both young and Latin like him. The two other guys veered off as Ricardo approached Jonas and me.

"Hey, Jonas, I get your call," he said. "You don't tell me you have such a *rico* friend."

Rico meant cute, baby-faced. Not the way I liked to be thought of. "I'm Angus," I said. "You must be Ricardo. Jonas has told me a lot about you. I'll have to see if it's all true."

He leaned in close to me. "Oh, yes, is all true." He ran a finger from my lips down my chin, down my chest, pulling away just before he reached my groin. I didn't have to fake the shiver of pleasure that shook me. "But first, you will buy me a drink? Tecate with a shot of Patron?"

I could see Jonas smirking, and remembered how he'd pointed out that I rarely bought drinks for myself. I was starting a new pattern. "Sure. Be right back."

I got the beer and tequila and when I returned, Ricardo was laughing with Jonas. Ricardo took the shot glass and tossed it back, then handed it to me like I was his personal valet, taking the beer with his other hand.

He wore a beautiful gold bracelet on his right wrist, and I took his arm and held it up to the light. I figured it was the one his married lover had given him back in Mexico.

"Very nice," I said. It was a simple band with a line of pavé diamonds in the center, with a gold seal on each end of the line, a circle with the letters G and L entwined.

"A gift from admirer," Ricardo said. "He work for company that make these." He held it up, and the tiny diamonds sparkled in one of the bar's spotlights.

I wore an entwined leather braid on my wrist, something I bought for myself at a flea market back in Pennsylvania. I made sure to keep it out of sight.

Ricardo and I talked and flirted for a while, and I wondered how I was going to get him to tell me anything. So I went back to those elicitation techniques I had studied at the academy. One of those was to make a statement that the subject knew was false, which would prompt him to refute it. "So, you used to work here?" I asked.

He shook his head. "No, not here. Lazy Dick's. You know it?"

"Sure. Jonas and I go there all the time." I knocked into my roommate. "How come you never introduced me to this guy before? You keeping him to yourself?"

"You get enough guys on your own," Jonas said, sullenly.

"So what do you do now?" I asked Ricardo. I tipped my own beer up and drank.

"I work for my cousin. Is much more responsibility. And you? What you do, Angus?" He pronounced my name with a Latin accent, like "an-goose."

"Accounting. Pretty boring."

He lifted his beer to drain the last dregs and the movement of his shirt sleeve revealed an angry, red bruise in the shape of Australia. "Wow. That must have hurt," I said, pointing to it.

Though I saw him wince as he put the empty bottle of Tecate on the table beside him, he said, "Was nothing. My cousin, she hits like a girl."

"Still, she must have been pissed at you."

"Was not my fault," he said. "She is angry I am not at the place where I work when something happen, but she is one who tell me go to Miami that day."

He looked like he was ready to stalk away. To keep him there, I asked, "Would you like another? Same again?" I finished my own beer.

"Sure." He handed me his empty bottle.

"I'll take a Heineken, as long as you're buying," Jonas said.

While I waited at the bar I parsed through what Ricardo had said. He wasn't at the place where he worked when something happened. The raid at the warehouse on Thursday? If she had sent him to Miami on an errand, that explained why there was no one at the bay when we arrived.

I ordered their drinks and another beer for myself, a Sam Adams cherry wheat.

His cousin had been angry, and had hit him, even though it wasn't his fault he wasn't there at the time.

I carried the drinks back, hooking the beers by their necks, and handed everything around. "So is your cousin okay with you being gay and all?"

"Is my business if I suck dick, nobody else's," Ricardo said. "She like pussy, I like dick. Is why we become close as cousins."

Then he leaned in next to me, breathing the smell of beer and tequila in my face, and said, in a low voice, "Except maybe you, Angus. You like me to suck your dick? You are so *rico*, and you are nice guy. You take care of your friends." He reached down and rubbed his hand against my crotch, and my dick stiffened.

I stammered, trying to think of something to say, when I was saved by Ricardo's cell phone ringing. He pulled it out of his pocket. "Is my cousin," he said, and he turned away from us to talk.

My Spanish was too basic to overhear anything. He said "*Sí*," a lot, then hung up. "I have to go," he said. He drained his beer.

There was nothing I could do to keep him there, and I'd already been warned against following someone on my own. I waited a couple of minutes to give him time to pull out of the parking lot, then I went outside and dictated everything I'd learned into my phone. It wasn't a lot, but as Roly had said before, it was another piece of the puzzle.

Would I be able to fill the missing pieces in before the jewelry show began? And if I did, what picture would it show?

19
BEST DAMN G-MAN

It was nearly 2:00 a.m., and I was beat, but the idea that Lester would get off work in an hour rejuvenated me.

He smiled broadly as I walked up to the door. He turned, leaned down to me, and cupped my face in his hands, then kissed me. It was one of those amazing, soul-deep kisses, his lips pressing against mine, electricity shooting between us. I wasn't tired after that. "Are you going home with me tonight?" he said into my ear.

"You bet." I ground my groin against his leg to show him just how happy I was to see him, and he smiled.

I went back to the bar, where Jonas was engaged in a deep, soulful conversation with a beefy bear-type who looked familiar. "Hey, you're the G-man," the guy said. "Lazy Dick's, the other day? You said you weren't dissing me, then you kissed me."

"Oh, yeah." I stuck out my hand. "I'm Angus. Jonas's roommate."

"Billy," the bear said.

"Jesus, Angus, is there any guy around here you haven't swapped spit with?" Jonas asked.

"Now, now, don't get jealous, doll," Billy said, putting his arm around Jonas's waist. "It was just a little peck on the cheek."

"Really?"

Billy pulled him close and kissed him, on the lips. I turned away to get my beer from the bartender, and when I turned back they were still kissing. "Come on you guys," I said, poking Jonas. "Keep it G-rated."

Billy pulled back and said, "Just so you know, doll, that was a kiss."

Jonas looked dazed. "It sure was," he said.

The bar started clearing out around two thirty. Jonas went off with Billy, holding his hand, and I helped Lester check all the doors and windows and lock the place up. We didn't leave the bar right away, though; we experimented with a couple of unique positions and settings. I hoped they gave the bar top a good washing down before they served food and drinks on it the next day.

I slept over at Lester's, and we stayed in bed all Sunday morning, eating Pop-Tarts and drinking bottled water, nibbling and nuzzling each other in between. Around noon we went to the fitness club together, and he put me through a hell of a workout—even more rigorous than we'd gone through the night before. I met a couple of his gym buddies and was embarrassed that I wasn't as pumped as any of them.

"Don't worry about bulking up," Lester said, when I admitted how I felt. "Every guy is different, and has different goals for his body. Come on, let me show you some yoga."

He led me into an empty dance studio at the gym, and I saw from the schedule on the wall there wouldn't be a class in there for another hour. "I can do the lotus," I said.

"Lot more to yoga than that."

We sat down on a mat, and I struggled to master a couple of simple asanas—though it was very hard for me to stay completely still. "You're strong but you need more flexibility," he said, forcing my arm to extend further.

"That's not what you said last night," I panted.

"Don't worry, I'll whip you into shape. You'll be the best damn G-man around when I get done with you."

"Who says I'm not that already?" I collapsed on the ground. "I don't see any of the other agents doing yoga."

He sat down next to me on the rubber mat. "That'll give you the advantage," he said. "You wait. Some yoga, tai chi, a couple of karate moves."

"You know all that stuff?" I looked at him, and at his reflection in all the mirrors. Damn, he was handsome and sexy.

"I know a lot." He stood up and reached down for my hand. "Come on, let's do some treadmill."

"You're a bastard," I said, but I took his hand and stood up. I did want to be the best damn G-man I could be.

After we finished our workout, I checked my voice mail and my Bureau e-mail to make sure I wasn't missing any developments in the case, but either nothing was happening, or I was already out of the loop. After an hour in the sauna and then a healthy low-cal dinner (yuck), he gave me a back rub, then sent me home so he could get ready for his shift at Equinox.

I tried Danny's cell as I drove home but got no answer.

Figured. The only time the kid wanted to talk to me was when I was in the middle of a case.

Jonas was home when I got there, wearing a satisfied smile. "So, you and Billy?" I asked.

"He's a sweetheart," Jonas said.

"That's it? I expect details." I flopped down on the living room sofa, across from him.

"You dish, I will."

I did. I told him about my night with Lester, in all its gory and delicious detail. He'd gone home with Billy, had some nice sex, and stayed the night. After breakfast at a diner, Billy had driven him home.

"How sweet," I said. "He sounds like a keeper."

"I don't know. I want to play the field for a while."

"Jonas. The guy's into you, he's sweet and cute and he doesn't charge. Stick with him."

"Fuck you, Angus. I only paid Ricardo once."

I looked at him.

"Well, twice. And a couple of his friends. You're right. I should hold on to Billy."

I was bone-tired, well-fucked and worked out, so I spent the rest of the evening on the couch watching TV with Jonas. I checked my e-mail and voice mail again, but there was nothing from Danny or anyone at the Bureau.

On Monday morning, I looked at the calendar and realized that the convention center trade show was starting on Thursday, and I still had nothing to go on other than a few random facts.

I created a new FD302 about my meeting on Saturday night with Ricardo, including all the notes I'd recorded at the bar after our conversation. As I worked, my desk phone rang and I answered, "Special Agent Green." Always gave me a little thrill to say that.

"My name is Hercules Dumond," he said. "Deputy with the Broward Sheriff's Office. Maria Fleitas told me she gave you my name."

"Yes, she did," I said.

"Which means you might have extended me the courtesy of telling me that you found the place where Francisco Gonzalez was murdered."

"Did the blood match?" I asked. I realized I hadn't thought to call the evidence techs to ask if they'd made the connection.

"Don't tell me you didn't know."

"I have bigger fish to fry than a simple murder," I said. "That's your job."

"A simple murder," he said. "That's all this man's life means to you?"

I took a deep breath. "No, that isn't what I meant. I've talked to a lot of people about Paco. I know he had a family back in Mexico, friends, a blue bicycle with purple Mardi Gras beads wrapped around the handlebars. I assure you I think of him as a real human being whose life was ended too soon."

"Then perhaps you'll be more willing to help me find out who did that," Dumond said. "If you know he went to that warehouse, tell me why, and who he was with."

"I can't tell you that. That individual may be involved in something much larger that has to take precedence."

"I need to hear that from someone with more authority than a special agent with less than six months in law enforcement under his belt."

How did Dumond know how new I was at the Bureau? Give the guy a few points for that. "I can get that to you ASAP."

"Please do if you ever want to have hope of working with the BSO in the future."

He hung up, and I thought about who'd have the juice to get Dumond to back off. The message was probably best coming from the SAC, but I didn't want to trample on anybody's toes by going to him directly. Instead I walked to Chris Potts's office.

She was on the phone, so I hovered in her doorway. She looked as if she hadn't gotten much sleep. "You're either the best agent I've seen in a dozen years or you have incredible luck," she said to me, when she hung up. "By getting a picture of Nilady Cruz at that storefront on Oakland Park Boulevard, you saved us about a month's worth of legwork figuring out where she was going to move next. We raided the place yesterday and found a lab in the back, where she's been manufacturing the White Persian."

"Wow," I said. "Yesterday." I was annoyed that I hadn't been in the loop about the raid, because I was the one who'd provided the tip, but that was the way things worked. The FBI was a collaborative effort. Individual agents researched cases, collected information, interviewed suspects, cultivated sources, and so on. Then we worked together as a team to make sure we had what we needed to make our cases, indict and convict our suspects.

If I was going to be a real agent, not just a desk jockey, I was going to have to get accustomed to that.

"Did you arrest Nilady Cruz? Her girlfriend?"

She shook her head. "The storefront was open but the

lab was closed, so there was no one back there. The desk clerks swore up and down they don't know who works there or how to reach them. We took fingerprints from the lab but we don't have prints for either Nilady Cruz or Vi Cunha in the system to match them."

It sounded like she was saying vicuna, the South American animal, and it took me a moment to realize that Ricardo's cousin Violeta went by Vi, and her last name was Cunha.

She sat back in her chair. "What took you out there, anyway?"

"I've been looking into Ricardo Cruz in conjunction with an investigation into a possible theft at a big jewelry show this week," I said. "I was talking to a source on Friday night, and he mentioned Ricardo had told him about a place to get pain pills."

"They do a word-of-mouth business," Chris said. "There's a surprisingly effective network of people addicted to oxycodone and other morphine derivatives. Of course, the dealers keep in contact with their clientele, too." She nodded. "Very sharp of you to pick up on that."

I thanked her, then told her about Hercules Dumond and his investigation into Paco's death. "I can't tell him about Ricardo Lopez without compromising your case. I know you wouldn't want him frightening off any of your suspects before you get your evidence together."

"Thanks. I'll make sure the SAC tells Dumond to back off for a while."

On my way back to my office, I made a detour past Vito's because I wanted some feedback on my next move. "I've been thinking. Paco Gonzalez worked for the food vendor at the convention center under a fake ID. That makes me think the company isn't very careful about checking paperwork, and that maybe that's the vulnerability—not so much the access points to the building."

He leaned back in his chair. "So whoever is behind this possible robbery is going to insert someone inside as a food worker? Interesting. How are you going to proceed?"

"I can't go to the concessionaire and ask for a list of all their employees without a warrant, right?"

Vito nodded.

"But I could approach them the same way I went to the security guy, right? Just tell them we've had word of a threat, and ask them how they vet their employees. See if I can identify any problems or holes. That would give us something to look at."

"Good idea. What else have you got?"

I thought for a minute. "I have a list of all the dealers who are coming to the show. I could look through the list and identify potential targets. But there are over three hundred companies on this list. How could I know which to focus on?"

"You ever been to one of these shows?" Vito asked.

"Nope."

"They get all different kinds of vendors. High-end, low-end, middle-price. People selling silver, gold, diamonds, and other precious stones. Look through your list and identify the people selling something worth stealing. Mostly that's diamonds, but with the price of gold these days that could be a target, too. And some of those weird gemstones can go for a million bucks a carat."

"But there are so many companies on this list. How am I going to get through them all in the next three days?"

"I suggest coffee. Lots of it."

Chained to a desk again. But at least I had some direction. The best damn G-man was on the case.

20
TROUBLES AND DREAMS

I found the website for Food Group International, the concessionaire at the Miami Beach Convention Center. I read about the various venues they had contracts with and clicked on the "apply online" link. They had all the right verbiage: you had to be authorized to work in the United States, have no criminal record less than five years old, and upload at least two forms of identification, including one photo ID issued by a government agency. You could also apply in person at offices in Fort Lauderdale or Miami.

Neither was close to the Bureau office in Miramar, but it was easier to get to the Lauderdale office. I hopped on the highway and found their office at the back end of a failed downtown mall called Riverwalk. Most of the stores and restaurants had been shuttered, which was a shame, because there was a nice promenade along the New River and the property was convenient to office, apartment, and condo towers. I climbed a winding staircase of terracotta tiles and followed signs to the back end of the property, where I found FGI's office tucked beyond the mall restrooms.

A fifty-something woman with tinted glasses and streaked blonde hair sat behind a desk with a cell phone to her ear and a bored look on her face. The metal placard in front of her read "Susan." She handed me a clipboard and said, "Fill out the front and back and provide two forms of ID."

There were three people in the waiting room filling out forms: two middle-aged Haitian women and a young white guy with tattooed arms.

I shook my head and palmed my ID. "Angus Green, FBI. I'd like to speak to someone in charge of hiring."

"I'll have to call you back," she said into her cell phone. Then she turned behind her and called, "Myra! The FBI is here!" The three applicants all looked up, and the white guy stood up, dropped his clipboard, and hurried out of the office.

Myra stepped out of the back office. She looked enough like Susan to be her sister. "How can I help you?" she asked, after she'd examined my badge.

She didn't offer to lead me in the back. "I'd like to discuss the way you vet the credentials of the people you hire."

"We do everything we're required to do by the law."

"I know for a fact that a man with falsified credentials worked at one of your venues."

"Hah!" she said, pointing a lacquered fingernail at me. "Worked! I assume he doesn't work for us anymore."

"That's correct. But I'd like to know how he got hired in the first place."

She shook her head. "Our attorneys have advised us that

we can't release any information about our past or present employees without a subpoena. Do you have one of those?"

"I do not."

"Then I can't help you."

"I'm not asking about specific employees," I said, keeping my voice even. "I just wanted to talk about your hiring practices in general."

"Read my lips, babycakes," Myra said. "Call my lawyer." She turned around and stalked back to her office, slamming the door behind her.

I was getting all kinds of new nicknames on this case—Agent Cutie Pie, now babycakes. "She always so friendly?" I asked Susan.

"Since she was born," she said. "Be glad she's my sister and not yours."

I made a mental note that FGI might merit some further investigation—anyone so quick to resist cooperation was often hiding something—and thanked Susan politely for her time, and her sister's.

Siblings. What can you do?

I drove back to the office and began going through the list of vendors, quickly eliminating all the ones who sold value-priced jewelry. It was a long, tedious process, but it was a lot better than anything I'd ever done behind a desk in Philadelphia.

There were nearly three hundred exhibitors, and most of them didn't even have websites. I had to depend on finding information about them secondhand, on listing services like the Yellow Pages and other aggregators. I managed to drop a lot of them off easily, because it was clear that they manufactured, imported, or sold cheap crap. But I was still left with close to a hundred companies that needed further investigation. It was going to be a long night.

Vito appeared in my office doorway around seven o'clock. His tie was loose and one of his shirt buttons was undone. "How you coming with your list?" he asked.

"Finished the first cut. I'm about halfway through the second run-through."

"Keep at it. Let's meet first thing tomorrow to go over what you've got."

"Sure thing."

A few minutes later Lester texted me. *U out 2nite?*

I texted back, *Got 2 work late, busy week. Back2u l8tr.*

He responded a couple of minutes later with *Yr loss*— followed by a frowning face.

Christine Potts was working late, too, so I got together with her around seven and we ordered a pizza to share. "Why are you here at this hour?" she asked, as we sat in the conference room to eat.

"Jewelry show on Thursday on Miami Beach. We got a tip that there might be a robbery there, and I'm wading through a mountain of data to identify potential targets."

My cell rang. "Cute ringtone," Chris said as Elton John's voice filled the room. "Your brother?"

"Yeah. Though I'm starting to wish I was an only child." I answered Danny's call. "What's up, bro? You find that credit card skimmer?"

"I'm not sure. I saw Rocket fiddling with a credit card last night and it looked like he was trying to swipe it through a machine like the one you told me about. But as soon as he saw me he put it away."

"That's excellent, Danny. You should get in touch with that cop, tell him what you saw."

"But what if I'm wrong? I don't want to throw Rocket under the bus."

"Then keep an eye on him. Get some more proof. If you can, take a picture of it, or of him using it."

"You're the best, Angus. I don't know what I would do if I didn't have you."

"You'd manage," I said. "I'll talk to you later."

"Your brother in trouble?" Chris asked as I put the phone back down on the table.

"Just in the middle of some drama," I said.

"I know that story," Chris said. "My little sister got pregnant at sixteen. Dropped out of high school, determined to raise the baby herself. Needless to say, my mom ended up taking care of the baby while Miriam worked a series of dead-end jobs. Eventually she took up with the wrong guy, started doing drugs, and got killed in a police raid on a crack house."

"Wow. That makes my brother's trouble seem like nothing."

She crunched the pizza box in half and stuffed it into the trash can. "I felt bad that I didn't do more for her—I was in college, then the academy, then caught up in my first job. By the time I looked up, it was too late. Don't let that happen to you."

I nodded. "Thanks."

I went back to my desk and kept going through my list. By ten o'clock I was down to a couple of vendors of high-end jewelry, the kind who might be bringing gold or precious gems to the show in enough quantity to interest a thief.

One name stood out. Gustavo Levy and Sons was a diamond merchant from Mexico City. Their website boasted connections to mines in South Africa and diamond cutters in Amsterdam. They catered to Mexico's richest customers.

There was something about the company and its logo that was familiar. But where had I seen it before? I wasn't a jewelry expert. I closed my eyes and tried to focus, but it was late, and I was tired.

I closed down my computer just before eleven and drove home, bone tired. Jonas wasn't home, and I hoped he was out with Billy the bear, having some fun. I stripped and climbed into bed, but even though I was exhausted, my brain wouldn't shut down.

My little brother needed me, and I couldn't go to him. All those years I had promised I would always be there for him, and now when he was in trouble I was putting my career first.

But what could I do up there? Hold his hand? He was a grown-up, and it was time he realized he had to act like one.

It made me wonder if Italy was really his dream. Or was it mine? Was I trying to force Danny to be somebody he didn't want to be? Maybe he didn't have the same dreams I had, after all. Maybe he was better off ending up like our dad, married and working an ordinary job.

Maybe I needed to stop dreaming for other people and focus on my own dreams. I finally drifted off, and slept until six thirty, when I woke up and went for a run around the neighborhood.

It was close to seven thirty when I finished my shower and started getting dressed. As I slipped on my leather bracelet I remembered how I'd hidden it from Ricardo, after seeing that beautiful gold and diamond one he wore.

Then it hit me. Ricardo had told me the bracelet was a gift from one of his admirers. The logo on his bracelet had matched the one from Gustavo Levy and Sons.

21
DEEP BREATH

I couldn't wait to get to the office and share what I had figured out with Vito. I zoomed south on 95 and then west on 595, darting around slow cars and trucks, nearly hitting one. I took a deep breath and willed myself to calm down. I wasn't going to do anyone any good if I was pancaked on the highway.

Vito wasn't in when I got there, so I called Navillus Sullivan. "I'm still working on a potential theft at the jewelry show. Right now I'm looking at a company called Gustavo Levy and Sons. What can you tell me about them?"

"Hold on. Let me bring up my database." I heard the sound of typing and some muffled cursing. "All right. Firm out of Mexico City. Three badges for the show: Jacobo, Baruch, and Moises Levy."

"You know how they're arriving here?"

"Nope. These high-end dealers are very cagey—don't want anyone to know when they're getting in, where they're staying. It's all part of the security. Often they'll make multiple reservations for flights and hotels, just to confuse anyone who might be tracking them."

I thanked him and hung up. If one of the Levy brothers had given Ricardo the bracelet, then I'd bet my badge that there was going to be a booty call at some point during the show. How would Ricardo and whichever Levy hook up?

I walked down the hall, looking for Vito. He still wasn't in, but Roly was. "Were you able to get the tap and trace for Ricardo Lopez's phone?"

He shook his head. "When he turned up in Chris Potts's case, I shifted everything to her. What do you need?"

I explained the situation to him. "I think Ricardo had, or maybe still has, a relationship with one of the Levy brothers," I said. "Which gives him some connection to the jewelry show."

"I've got a contact with the Mexican *Policía Federal Ministerial*," he said.

I loved the way he switched into a Spanish accent for things like that.

"They're pretty much our equivalent. I'll send him an e-mail and see if he knows anything about the company. Check with Chris and see if she has surveillance on Lopez already."

I thanked him and found Chris Potts. She looked a lot better that morning, like she'd gotten a good night's sleep. "Lopez has gone underground, along with his cousin and Nilady Cruz," she said. "We've had the house where they were living staked out, but no one has shown up there since the raid. No activity on any of their known cell phones or internet accounts, either."

"I saw him Saturday night at a bar, but I didn't follow him when he left because I was on my own, and I didn't realize you were looking for him. But I might have a way to find him." I explained about the connection to the Levy brothers and the jewelry show. "If we follow the brothers, one of them might lead us to Ricardo. But right now this is my only real lead on the potential theft, so I need Ricardo to stay in play for a while."

"He's small potatoes to me," Chris said. "I can give you a little rope. But if either Vi Cunha or Nilady Cruz show up, I'll have them arrested in a New York minute."

"Understood," I said.

Back at my office I did some basic research on the three brothers. From an article in a jewelry magazine online, I discovered that that all three were Orthodox Jews; their grandfather, a skilled jeweler, had immigrated to Mexico from Poland during World War II. His son Gustavo had established the family business in 1985.

Their business was importing raw stones, including emeralds, amethysts, topazes, and diamonds, from various countries in South America, primarily Brazil. They cut them precisely, using gemologists trained in Amsterdam, then sold them to jewelers around the world. They operated out of a large, modern facility in the Condesa neighborhood of Mexico City, and their company was often represented at wholesale jewelry shows.

The company's spokesman was the youngest son, Moises. He had gone to business school in the United States, then returned to Mexico City to join the family firm. I couldn't find much else about him, or the rest of his family, online on my own.

"How's it going, rookie?"

Vito loomed in my office door, holding a venti-sized coffee. Even early in the morning he looked sloppy, with one button open in the middle of his shirt, and one corner of his shirt pulling out of his pants.

"I made some progress," I said.

He sat down, and I told him about Ricardo's bracelet, and matching the logo on it to the Levy firm. "Good work. It could be coincidence, but probably not. We're going to need to set up surveillance on the show floor. We might as well focus on the Levy booth, since that's the best lead we've got. Let's see the layout."

"We should also keep an eye on the food operation," I said. "Since that's where Paco worked, and he was your original source." I told him about how uncooperative Myra at FGI had been.

"Not surprising," he said. "People with papers don't want to work those shit jobs." He shook his head. "America was built on the backs of immigrants. My grandparents, Roly's parents, somebody somewhere in your family, I'm sure. They come here, willing to do whatever they can to make a better life. It's criminal what the government does these days." He held up his hands, palms out. "But don't get me started."

I opened up the printed show program Sullivan had given me. "All one big hall," Vito said. "That's good. Easy control of access in and out of the room."

"There's the Levy booth," I said, pointing. It was about two-thirds of the way down one aisle, on the north side of the show.

Vito put his thumb and forefinger down on the diagram

and measured, swinging his hand around. "Any one of these four booths. We need to set up in a position where we can watch what's going on."

"Do we tell the Levy brothers they're a target? If we do, we can ask them what kind of security they have in place."

"We'll connect with them at some point. In the meantime, get hold of your guy and get us set up in one of these booths."

As soon as he left, I called Navillus Sullivan and explained what I needed. "What are you basing this on?" he asked.

"I can't get into details. But I can tell you we feel there is a credible threat to the firm during the show."

"I'll have to make some calls and get back to you."

While I waited I went back over the list of show vendors. I checked for those who were near the Gustavo Levy booth, for other vendors of high-end merchandise, and buyers and sellers from Mexico. Nothing I came up with looked as logical as an attempt on the Levy brothers.

My e-mail program burped. Roly had not only attached a file with information from his contact in Mexico, but he'd gotten hold of flight reservations the brothers had made.

I began with the PDFs the Mexican agent had attached—one for each of the brothers. I was surprised he had been able to put them together so quickly, and wondered if his agency already had dossiers on each of the brothers—and if so, why.

Because it was the easiest way to approach them, I began alphabetically, with Baruch. He owned a home in Condesa, close to his office, as well as a condominium in Puerto Vallarta, on the Pacific coast. He was married to a woman named Sofia and had two sons, Gustavo and Benjamin, who attended private school. He and his brothers owned equal shares in the business. I scanned quickly through his tax returns, but they were all in Spanish, and I'd never taken any coursework in international taxation, so most of it was incomprehensible to me.

I yawned. This was the kind of boring research I hated, the reason why I hadn't wanted to go into public accounting. I got myself another cup of coffee and started on Jacobo.

He was nearly a clone of his older brother. He'd gone to the same schools, and lived only a couple of blocks away. He owned a condo in the same building in Puerto Vallarta. He had a wife whose name was Elisa, and a son named Gustavo. The only way he'd deviated was in having a daughter named Gabriella. What a wacky guy.

He was only slightly less prosperous than his brother. He and his family belonged to the same synagogue as his brother's, and his kids attended the same school as their cousins.

The baby brother was Moises. His wife's name was Miriam, and what do you know? He had only one child—a son named Gustavo. Give him time, I guess. He had a condo in Puerto Vallarta, too.

I sat back in my chair. How could you keep track of all those kids with the same name? Then I remembered one of my college roommates, a Jewish guy from Philadelphia. Ashkenazi Jews, he told me, were the ones from Russia and Poland, and they named their children after the dead. The Sephardim, like his family, were descended from those kicked out of Spain by Ferdinand and Isabella. They had spread around the Mediterranean, to North Africa, Italy, Turkey, and Greece. They named their children after the living—usually after grandparents. That explained why all the boys were named Gustavo.

My roommate's name was Aaron, and he had three male cousins with the same name. But each one had a different Spanish nickname, and he hadn't realized his name wasn't Chucho until he went to kindergarten.

I went back to Moises's file and scanned through his tax returns, not paying much attention until something jumped out at me. In addition to his other assets, he owned a house in a small town in Pennsylvania called Milford. I'd never heard of the place, so I looked it up on Google Maps. It was along the Delaware River, nestled at the head of the Delaware Water Gap. A strange place for an Orthodox Jew from Mexico to have a vacation home, especially when he was the only one of the brothers to have done so.

I put aside the research from the Mexican cop and went back to what Roly had found. All three brothers had reservations from Mexico City to Miami for a flight arriving the next day at 9:30 a.m. They also all had reservations for a flight arriving on Thursday morning at the same time.

Moises had a third reservation, for an Aeroméxico flight that arrived the next day at 4:30 p.m. Jacobo and Baruch had seats on a flight arriving later that night, at 10:25. I printed the e-mail and circled the 4:30 flight. If I were Moises and I was planning to hook up with Ricardo, I'd take a flight that got in before my brothers' and give them a bogus reason why.

Sullivan called back a while later. One of the vendors in a booth across from the Levy brothers had cancelled at the last minute, so we could use that space for our surveillance. Since almost every trade show had a few generic vendors along with the ones related to that industry, we'd had a fake booth made that would fit in almost anywhere. I put in a request to have it retrieved and shipped out to the conference center.

After that I figured that, since I had been trained as a number cruncher, I ought to crunch some numbers. How much money would usually change hands at a trade show like the one on Miami Beach? What was the average value of the diamonds that a company like Gustavo Levy and Sons would carry? I wanted to be sure that robbing the brothers would net the bad guys enough money to be worth the trouble.

I ran scenarios and speculations until my eyes were crossed. When I looked up, Vito Mastroianni was standing in my doorway.

"Go home, rookie," he said. "Get a good night's sleep. You'll need it tomorrow."

I couldn't just quit. There was always something else I could research, some other contingency I could plan for. I took Vito's advice, shut down my computer, and walked through the empty corridors of the office, but I kept picking at the problem in front of me.

I picked up a salad, a bottle of Guinness, and a pint of vanilla ice cream at Whole Foods. Ate my salad at the kitchen table, feeling virtuous, then made myself a milkshake out of the beer and the ice cream. I was excited about the next day, determined to prove my mettle. I refused to even consider any possibility of failure. The next day would show the world that Angus Green was ready for anything the bad guys could come up with.

22
BOOTY CALL

I met the shipping team at the convention center Wednesday morning. It was a scene of controlled chaos: trucks waiting in line to unload, police competing to direct traffic. The air was filled with the sounds of hammers, power drills, and cell phone ringtones. I had a headache after half an hour.

Our booth was a front for an operation selling land in North Carolina. The back and sides were panoramic photos of sparkling lakes, verdant green hills, and cloudless blue skies. I wanted to pick up and move there immediately, which I guess was the point. I unpacked a box of flyers advertising lakefront lots that would "soon" be available at "market" prices. There was an 800 number and a website address.

"What do I do if someone asks about property?" I asked the guy from the shipping department, who was setting up the panels.

"Most people won't even pay attention to you," the guy said. "If they ask, you just tell them you're temporarily on hold for land sales. They can take a brochure and check back on the website in a month or two."

Sounded dumb to me, but I hoped the guy was right. I walked around the floor getting a sense of the layout, and I was relieved to see that ours wasn't the only non-jewelry operation. A cell phone company was down the aisle from us, and an investment planning group was around the corner.

I began at the rear of the big hall, where a dozen tables clustered behind roped-off stanchions. Four empty steam tables protected by sneeze guards stood to one side; a rack had already been filled with snacks. A refrigerated case held cold drinks, premade salads, and fruit cups. A fancy soda machine dispensed a couple of dozen variations on popular brands, from diet to caffeine-free to fruit-flavored.

Navillus Sullivan approached as I looked around. "Morning, Agent Green," he said. "Find any security breaches?"

I reached out to shake his hand. "Not yet. But the morning's still young."

He grinned. "Not a very impressive setup," he said, waving his hand. "Some of the shows bring in gourmet caterers."

"Where's the food prep?"

"Off-site," he said. "There's a staging area behind those doors, adjacent to the loading dock. Take a walk with me, and I'll show you the cart positions."

We began a clockwise circuit of the building. Carts serving bottled water, energy drinks, power bars, and prewrapped sandwiches were stationed around the room. A young woman in an apron with the FGI logo on it would man each cart. "The cart operators are in radio contact with a supply depot in the back, and a man with a hand truck will bring them supplies as they need."

I didn't say anything to Sullivan, but I could see a dozen ways that someone could sabotage the food supply. I could offer to get someone a soda, for example, and slip a roofie into the cup as the machine dispensed it. I could put a chemical into a hypodermic needle and inject it into a shrink-wrapped sandwich. If someone had an allergy to nuts, I could sprinkle powdered peanuts over a salad.

But all I could do at that point was be vigilant. I thanked Sullivan for his help and went back to the booth. By noon it was complete, though most of the others around us were still under construction. I was glad to get out of the madhouse and drive to Miramar in my quiet, air-conditioned car.

While I waited for my computer to boot up, I called my brother. The call went straight to voice mail, which meant that either he was on the phone, his battery had run down, or he was just ignoring me. Or maybe he was in police custody. At that point I had no idea.

"Hey, bro. Give me a call when you can. I want to make sure you're all right. I love you." Then I hung up.

I looked up to see Roly in my doorway.

"What's going on?" he asked.

"My brother's in trouble." He came into my office and sat down, and I explained the story to him. I tried to put into words the conflict I was feeling. "I wish I could fly up there and sort things out for him, but he's got to learn to stand on his own, right? I can't keep fixing his problems all his life."

"Family's the most important thing," he said. "It's why I won't take a promotion in the Bureau. Can't leave Miami. Look at Vito. Tears him up every time something happens back in Jersey with his family." Vito didn't seem like the sentimental type to me, but then again, I didn't know him all that well.

My computer was up by then, and I checked to make sure Moises Levy had caught that flight from Mexico City. Yup. I was almost certain he was headed for a booty call with Ricardo Lopez. I swiveled the screen around to show Roly. "Moises Levy is on the Aeroméxico flight," I said, eager to get back onto the case and away from my brother's troubles. "It's in the air. I want to go out to the airport and see if Ricardo Lopez shows up to meet him, or if Levy goes directly to his hotel."

"Good idea. But Lopez knows that Mini Cooper of yours. So you'd better check out a car from the Bureau vehicle pool. And you'll need backup. Get Vito to go with you."

He walked away, and after I had texted Vito a request for backup, I sat back in my chair. Something kept nagging at the back of my mind. There was a detail I'd missed. What was it? I went back over everything I'd done that day. I couldn't come up with anything.

Was it something in my research on the Levy brothers? Had I been too quick to skim over their tax records? I was a trained accountant, after all. I forced myself to go back to the information on Moises and read through it all again.

Once more, the choice of Milford, Pennsylvania stuck out. Why there? Moises had gone to business school at Wharton, but Milford was way outside Philly, three hours up the Delaware. I pulled up a map of the town. Was there a cluster of Orthodox Jews there?

I googled the terms together and got no hits. Then I googled "Milford" and "gay," and, what do you know,

Milford was a lower-key version of New Hope, the artists' colony along the Delaware that had long been a haven for gay men. Milford would be perfect for a guy on the down low who wanted to sneak away for a weekend now and then.

I looked at my watch and realized I had to get a move on. I trekked out to where the Bureau vehicles were, and checked out a nondescript Ford Taurus. I cranked up the air-conditioning full blast and switched the radio to some classic rock as I crept along in traffic to Miami International Airport.

While I was stuck at a light, I texted Danny: *Talk to me, bro.*

Moises's plane was due in at 4:30. He'd have to clear customs, which could take a couple of hours. If I were Ricardo, I'd hang around near the airport, and have Moises call as he was just about finished and ready to be picked up—which would probably be around 6:30 or so.

I circled around the cell phone waiting lot. No sign of Ricardo's SUV. I played word games on my phone to keep my brain going, looking up every minute or two to make sure I wasn't missing anything. Every time the game was slow I kept hoping it was because the phone was about to receive a call or text, but no such luck.

Vito called around six to say that he was on his way to the airport. "What if we're wrong, and Ricardo doesn't meet Moises Levy?" I asked.

"Then we focus on tomorrow. You got the booth all set up? It's just going to be you and me, so we'll have to take turns going to the john, getting lunch, and walking around."

About fifteen minutes later, I saw Ricardo's SUV enter the lot and slide into a spot a few cars beyond me. I slouched down in my seat, but he didn't seem to have noticed me.

I called Vito. "Ricardo's here," I said. "In the cell phone lot."

"I'm right behind you," he said. I glanced into my rear view mirror and sure enough, there he was, gliding past. He took a spot a few rows down from mine. "Just spoke to a buddy of mine in customs. Levy's passport was scanned about five minutes ago. So he should be making his booty call any minute now."

23
FAMILY REUNION

Ricardo backed out of his parking spot a few minutes later. I waited a couple of beats and then followed him to Terminal F. When he pulled up and put on his flashers, I parked a couple of cars behind him.

A slim man in his early thirties towing a rolling suitcase came out of the sliding glass doors, and Ricardo beeped his horn. The man raised his right hand and waved, and strode over to the SUV. He wore a perfectly tailored gray suit, black dress shoes, and a white shirt with a red tie. His black hair was short and slick. When he stopped to load his suitcase in the back of the SUV, I got a glimpse of his face.

He was quite handsome, in a well-groomed way, and I wondered why he was bothering with a low-life hustler like Ricardo Lopez. Was he that deep in the closet that he had to pay for sex, and Ricardo was all he could find?

"I've got Ricardo," I said to Vito. "It looks like Moises

Levy just came out of the terminal and he's getting into the SUV."

"I'm pulling into the terminal now. I'll pick up his tail, and you hang back."

Vito followed Ricardo out of the airport and onto the 112, heading east. Once we were all on the highway, Vito dropped back, and I took the lead, staying a few cars back as we headed across the palm-lined Julia Tuttle Causeway to Miami Beach.

There was still enough light that I could see expanses of Biscayne Bay to the north and south, the landscape a mix of Spanish-tile roofs on single-family homes, glassy condo towers glittering in the fading sun, and a smattering of sailboats on the smooth surface of the bay. Times like that made me marvel at the luck that had brought me to such a beautiful place.

Vito and I alternated following the SUV south on Collins Avenue, the road that paralleled the beach, past a phalanx of sixties-era condo towers, to the oceanfront Loews Hotel in the center of South Beach. Ricardo left his SUV with the valet and followed Moises into the hotel. "I'll sit out here while you park," Vito said. "Then you come back here prepared to follow on foot if you have to."

It took me a couple of minutes, as parking around South Beach always does, but I pulled into a spot in the public garage across the street and hopped out of the car. "I'm on foot," I said to Vito. "Any sight of them?"

"Nope. I'm parked at a hydrant on Collins in view of the hotel. You go into the lobby and ask to speak to hotel security. See if Levy checked in."

"Will do." From the garage, I crossed Collins, noting

where Vito was parked, and walked through the luxurious lobby to the concierge desk. "Good evening. My name is Angus Green and I'm an agent with the FBI." I showed the elegantly coiffed Jamaican woman behind the desk my badge. "I'd like to verify if a guest has checked in yet. Can you do that for me, or do I need to speak to security?"

"I can check for you, sir. May I have the guest's name?"

"Moises Levy. Would have happened just a few minutes ago."

She typed at her keyboard, then looked up. "Room 2125. He's scheduled to stay until Sunday."

I smiled. "Thank you very much."

"Is he in trouble? Should I notify hotel security?"

"Just routine," I said, and walked away.

I called Vito and told him what I'd learned. "Stake out the lobby," he said. "Find a spot with a view of the elevators. But if I were you I'd hit the head first, so you don't have to when it's not possible."

"Thanks for the hint." I followed his advice, then got a bottle of water from the convenience shop and a copy of *USA Today* and sat in the lobby.

The end-of-day people-watching was fun. Families trailed in from the pool, little kids wrapped in towels, moms with big sunglasses, dads in T-shirts and flip-flops. Men and women attending a convention in the building streamed through, their name tags around their necks. A group of Japanese tourists, each one with a camera, chattered to each other and smiled a lot.

Baby boomer rock played through the stereo system, and the air smelled like orchids and salt water. I finished my bottle of water after the first hour but didn't get another, wary of Vito's warning. Another hour passed, with no sign of Ricardo or Levy. What were they doing up there? Well, I knew. But either they both had awesome staying power, or they were taking a nap.

If I were Moises Levy, though, I wouldn't doze off with Ricardo Lopez around. He might wake up missing his watch, wallet, and whatever jewelry he was carrying to the show.

It was almost nine o'clock when Ricardo came down to the lobby. I called Vito's cell. "Ricardo's downstairs, but he's alone. What do we do? Follow him or stay on the hotel?"

"We should talk to Mr. Levy," Vito said. "Wait there. I'll park and come in."

I went back to my seat, keeping an eye on the elevator bank. A few minutes later, Moises Levy stepped out. I called Vito. "Levy is on the move. He's at the car rental desk in the lobby."

"Fuck me, I just parked. Stay on him, watch the car he gets into. I'll get back in position."

The young guy behind the rental desk moved like he had just woken up from a very long siesta. Levy didn't seem to mind; I saw him joking with the clerk, probably flirting with him. The clerk picked up the phone and spoke to someone, then handed Levy a sheaf of paperwork.

The Mexican thanked him and walked toward the front door. I hung back, pretending to read a brochure about airboat rides through the Everglades. A bright red Toyota sedan pulled up, and a valet hopped out. Levy handed him a piece of paper and then got behind the wheel. I called Vito and read him the plate number and a description of the vehicle.

"Call me when you get in your car," Vito said, and disconnected.

A heavy hand landed on my shoulder as I turned to leave. "I'd like to know what you're doing, sir."

I slipped away from the hand's grip and pivoted to see a burly guard in a hotel security uniform. "Agent Green, FBI." I held up my right hand. "Reaching for my badge."

I slipped it out of my pocket and showed him. "Good to see you guys are on your toes. Gotta run."

I hurried out the front door, sprinting down the drive and across Collins Avenue between cars. I was in my car a minute later, waiting while an old lizard in an ancient Buick fiddled for money to pay the attendant.

"I'm in line to leave the garage," I said, when Vito picked up the phone. "Where are you?"

"Heading south on Collins in heavy traffic. Our boy isn't going anywhere fast."

By the time I got out of the garage, Levy had turned east on Fifth Street as if he were heading for the causeway back to Miami. I detoured down Alton Road and was able to catch up to him and Vito on the 836.

We played our cat-and-mouse game with him all the way to the airport. "This is getting very familiar," Vito said. "I checked the flight manifests while I was waiting. His brothers are both on the flight that landed at 10:25. The guy I know at customs is off duty by now, so I won't be able to find out when their passports are swiped."

It didn't matter; Moises Levy headed right back to Terminal F and pulled up in the pickup lane in front of a pair of middle-aged men. "Looks like the Levy brothers are having a family reunion," I said to Vito.

I pulled past them and let Vito pick up the trail, driving slowly back toward the causeway. By the time I had reached it, Vito let me know that the red Toyota was moving again.

"I think they're going back to the hotel," he said. "I'm going to head over there, park, and wait for them in the lobby. You follow them, park, and then call me."

I did as I was told. Fortunately Moises Levy was a sedate driver, by Miami standards, and I had no trouble keeping him in view. Instead of going back to the hotel, though, he stopped at an off-airport rental company. I was worried they'd split up, and I'd be screwed—but both his brothers got similarly non-descript cars and like good little ducklings all three of them drove back to the Loews in a row.

This time I was lucky and got a space right inside the entrance to the garage. I sprinted back across the street and up the driveway to the lobby. The security guard I'd spoken to earlier was nowhere in sight, but Vito was standing by the elevators.

I crossed the lobby toward him as he intercepted the Levy brothers. He showed his badge, and when I reached him he was saying, "We'd like to talk to you, if you have a few minutes."

Baruch was heavier and rounder, Jacobo more angular, with pointy eyebrows. In Moises, these features combined harmoniously. He'd removed his suit jacket and his tie, opened his collar, and rolled the sleeves of his shirt up to his elbows. Around his neck he wore a hand-crafted Star of David on a heavy gold chain.

"What this is about?" Moises asked, with a Spanish accent that was much less pronounced than I had expected.

Vito nodded toward me. "Agent Green and I have

some questions about the jewelry show, and we have some information to share with you."

Baruch said, "We will listen," and led us toward a group of chairs by the tall windows that looked out at the hotel next door. All three brothers wore a lot of jewelry—gold watches, heavy gold bracelets, wedding bands, and pinky rings set with precious stones.

"Two weeks ago we received a tip concerning a possible robbery at the jewelry show," Vito said. "Your company has come up in our investigation as potential victims."

"We take our security very seriously," Baruch said. His accent was much heavier than his brother's, but still understandable. "My brothers and I each carry identical briefcases. We travel together whenever possible, but when we are separated there is no way for anyone to know which one of us carries the merchandise."

Vito nodded. "Agent Green, do you have the photo of Ricardo Lopez?"

I pulled out the picture I had taken from Lazy Dick's, the one with Paco, Ricardo, and Jonas, and showed it to the three men. "Do you know any of these men?" I asked.

"They look like homosexuals," Baruch said with distaste. "We would not know any of them."

I kept my eyes on Moises, but he didn't show a flicker of recognition.

"Does one of these men think he can rob us?" Jacobo asked.

"We're not sure," Vito said. "But we wanted to give you a heads-up. We're going to be watching you during the show, just as a precaution."

"Watching us? What do you mean?" Moises asked.

Vito explained about the surveillance. "You think this is necessary?" Jacobo asked.

Vito nodded. "We believe so, yes."

"Then it is good you will do it." Baruch smiled. "Do you need anything from us?"

"No. But if you see us at the show, please don't call attention to us." He handed each of the men his card. "Here's my cell number. If you see anything suspicious or feel threatened at all, call me."

The three brothers took the cards, then thanked us and walked toward the elevator banks.

"What do we do now?" I asked Vito.

He looked at his watch. It was well after midnight by then. "Let's rendezvous at the convention center booth tomorrow at eight. You have my credentials?"

I handed him the pass I'd picked up that morning when I set up the booth. "What if Ricardo has something planned for tomorrow morning?" I asked. "Shouldn't we stick to the Levy brothers?"

"You heard what they said. They've got a security plan for travel to and from the show. And Ricardo, or whoever else is behind this, wouldn't have needed the convention center plans if they were going to hit the guys outside."

"You're the boss," I said.

"Yeah, tell my wife that. See you tomorrow."

24
SHOWTIME

After I left South Beach, I had to drive back to the office and swap out the motor-pool car for my own. I was too tired to call or text Danny again, and by the time I got home Wednesday night it took all my energy to strip and crash. When I woke early the next morning, I'd hardly slept.

I was buzzing, my head full of details of the case, and I didn't have a spare brain cell to think about my brother or his problems. Besides, wherever he was, I was sure he was still asleep. I dressed in a suit, one that was baggy enough to hide my Kevlar vest underneath. By the time I pulled into the parking lot across from the center, it was half full. I made sure to get a spot on the end, so I could pull out easily if I had to follow someone.

Security guards stood at the single door into the big room, and they seemed to be doing a good job of checking IDs and controlling access to the show. When I got to the booth Vito was already there, holding a venti-sized coffee and a bear claw, and I was sorry I hadn't stopped to get my own caffeine on the way in.

The morning moved at a glacial pace. I kept stealing glances at my cell phone in case Danny was trying to get hold of me, but there was nothing. I texted him again anyway. Vito and I sat at the booth, ignoring anyone who showed any interest, focusing our attention on the Levy brothers across the way. They had a steady stream of customers, and most of the transactions went on in the back of the booth, where one of the brothers was always sitting at a small round table looking at jewelry and gem stones.

Vito took a walk around the convention center, checking to make sure there was nothing unusual going on. While he was gone I saw a guy who looked familiar, strolling down the aisle and heading toward the Levy booth.

I ran through my mental data bank. Who was he? I knew I'd seen him somewhere. He was in his forties, trim in a rangy, cowboy sort of way, in a plaid shirt with mother-of-pearl buttons, Levis 401 jeans, and worn leather boots. It was the twirly mustache that finally rang a bell. His name was Peter, and at the Equinox he'd been playing pool, and playing footsie in the men's room, with Ricardo Lopez.

I called Vito's cell. "Where are you? We've got a situation back here at the booth."

"I'm one aisle over. Be right there."

For a big guy, Vito moved fast through a crowd. "What's the situation?" he said, hurrying into the booth, carrying a super-sized drink in one hand and a half-eaten breakfast burrito in the other.

"That cowboy coming down the aisle? The one with the

handlebar mustache? I saw him playing pool with Ricardo Lopez at the Equinox."

"And?"

"And I think they were having sex in the men's room."

He looked at me. "And?"

"Don't you see? They could be in some kind of conspiracy!"

Vito sighed. "Sit down, rookie." He took a long slurp of soda and a bite of his burrito. In the meantime, Peter stopped at a booth selling all kinds of cheap costume jewelry, including strands of brightly colored Mardi Gras beads, and began examining the merchandise.

"Oh, my God," I said. "Mardi Gras beads. The same kind of beads that were wrapped around Paco's handlebars."

"Angus. Get a grip. Not everything in the world is a conspiracy. You have any evidence at all that this guy has been in contact with Ricardo Lopez about anything other than some bathroom boogie?"

I felt like a misbehaving teenager. "No."

"You ever talk to that guy at the bar?"

"Yeah. We played pool once."

"He know you're a fed?"

I shook my head. "Okay. We'll watch him, see what happens when he passes the Levys. Then, if you want, you can go up to him. Hey, funny running into you here. You interested in some land in North Carolina? See how it goes."

I felt a little better. "Thanks, Vito."

"Hey, I've seen some crazy shit in this job. You never know."

We sat down, and watched Peter place an order for Mardi Gras beads. Then he bought some blinking bracelets from another booth, bypassing anything with a retail price greater than ten bucks. He walked right past the Levys without giving them a second glance. I got up circled around the next aisle, and on my way back to the booth I made sure to intersect him.

"Hey, Peter, right?" I said. "I'm Angus. We played pool at the Equinox the other night."

"As I recall you played with Enrique," he said, shaking my outstretched hand. "I watched." He looked me up and down. "You've been working out. Put some more meat on your bones since I last saw you."

That had to be the vest under my jacket—not the workout I'd had with Lester on Sunday. "You're in the jewelry business?" I asked.

He shook his head. "I own a store on Wilton Drive. Cards, novelty items, calendars, gay stuff. I pick up a few things here—glow in the dark bracelets and shit." He pulled out a plastic bead. "See these? Stick 'em on your ear, people think you've got gauges."

I shuddered, unsure why someone would want those huge holes in their earlobes.

"How about you?" Peter asked.

"Right now I'm working for a company that sells land in North Carolina. But they've got some kind of legal snafu, so we can't actually sell anything. Boring just sitting around."

"I hear you. I had a bunch of those kind of jobs when I was young and cute like you."

"Listen, I've got to get back to the booth. My boss'll dock me if I'm away too long. See you at Equinox sometime."

"Any time you get tired of hanging around with Lester, you come look me up," he said, and smiled.

I smiled back, and walked away. I remembered what Jonas had said, about my never having to pay for drinks. I guess I wasn't as inconspicuous as I thought.

"You were right," I said, when I got back to the booth. "No connection to Ricardo."

By then it was lunchtime. Vito and I alternated getting our lunches, and over the next hour, we watched as the three Levy brothers each got up to get their own food, one at a time. They even staggered their bathroom breaks. Around two, though, Jacobo made two trips to the men's room in quick succession. When he returned from the second trip, he looked green. Vito got up and intercepted him before he could go back into the booth.

When he returned to me, Vito said, "Something he ate didn't agree with him. He's going back to the hotel."

"What was it?"

Vito shrugged. "He's the one who speaks the least English, so I couldn't figure it out."

"This isn't good, Vito. Remember, Paco worked for the food service people. Someone could have figured out some way to poison his food. He should be going to the hospital, not back to his hotel."

"Hold on, rookie. There's no reason why anyone would poison him."

"It could be a way to split them up," I said. "Remember they told us about their security measures? How no one ever knows which brother has the case with the jewelry? If Jacobo leaves, then that's only two brothers left to play swap the case."

"Possibility," Vito said. "We'll keep an eye on the other two."

I looked across the aisle, to where Baruch and Moises were both meeting with clients. Neither of them looked sick. Maybe Jacobo's illness was just a coincidence.

I might end up looking like a fool, but I'd be a thorough fool. When Baruch finished with his customer, I darted across the aisle and intercepted him. "Sorry to bother you, but what did you eat for lunch?" I asked.

"Tuna fish sandwich," he said. "Why?"

"Do you know what your brothers ate?"

He looked curiously at me. "Because Jacobo got sick? We all keep kosher, Agent Green. So we all ate the same thing. A tuna fish sandwich, a bag of potato chips fried in vegetable oil, and a bottle of water."

"From the same cart?"

"Yes. The one right back there." He motioned to the closest corner. The cart looked abandoned.

"Thanks," I said. "Sorry to bother you."

He smiled. "I appreciate your efforts to look out for me and my brothers."

I walked down the aisle to the cart. The attendant was nowhere in sight, though there was still a lot of merchandise on the display. I called Navillus Sullivan and asked if he knew where the attendant had gone. "Didn't realize she wasn't there," he said. "I'll get somebody from FGI over there."

I waited at the cart until the supervisor arrived. She was a heavyset Haitian woman with a thick accent. "These girls, they don't want to work," she said. "This one, this her first job. She probably get bored and just walk away." She shook her head and radioed for someone to come remove the merchandise and lock up the cart.

"Can you give me the name of the girl who was working here?"

"You got to get that from the office," she said. "Myra don't let anybody give out information."

Great. Back to Myra. I already knew how helpful she was.

I went back to the land sales booth, where Vito was sitting on a folding chair arguing on his cell phone with his daughter about doing her homework. I sat next to him and watched the Levy brothers' booth.

With Jacobo gone, Moises and Baruch struggled to keep up with the volume of appointments and walk-up traffic, and I wondered if this was part of the plan—get the remaining brothers so distracted that they would drop their guard and allow someone to walk away with valuable merchandise.

By four o'clock Vito and I were both yawning. I hadn't heard anything from Danny, and the stress of worrying about him was wearing me down as much as the Levy case. "The coffee in this place sucks," Vito said. "The show has another hour to run, so our boys aren't moving until then. You want to make a Starbucks run? There's two of them on Lincoln Road."

"With pleasure. I'll even buy your coffee."

He gave me his order, and I walked outside. It was a gorgeous day, blue skies, a light breeze, and temperatures in the upper seventies. It would have been downright comfortable if I hadn't had the Kevlar vest on under my shirt. I took my time walking to Lincoln Road, enjoying the brief break.

I got my coffee and Vito's and walked back to the convention center. As I was crossing Seventeenth Street, I caught sight of Ricardo Lopez coming out of the garage, just to my left. I stepped back against the wall of the garage and watched him cross the street.

I put one of the coffee cups on the top of a trash can and called Vito. "I have eyes on Ricardo Lopez," I said. "On Seventeenth Street, about a block from the convention center."

"Stay on him and let me know where he goes."

I left Vito's coffee behind on the trash can and followed Ricardo across the street and up to the front of the convention center.

Instead of going inside, though, he continued walking. Where was he going? Did he have some kind of ambush set up for the Levy brothers? I stepped under the overhang of the convention center and watched him walk. He strolled to the end of the building, crossed the access road, and leaned up against the wall of the Miami Botanical Garden. He pulled a cigarette out of his pocket and lit up.

I called Vito again. "Lopez is standing outside smoking a cigarette."

Vito nodded. "That explains the call Moises just got. He looked awful damned happy to get it."

"What do we do? You want me to stay out here and keep an eye on Ricardo?"

Vito shook his head. "He knows you. It would be too easy for him to make you. It's almost the end of the day. Come on back in, and we'll keep an eye on the brothers instead."

I gave Vito my coffee, because I'd left his behind, and fidgeted for the next hour as the Levy brothers finished their negotiations for the day. By five o'clock the booths around us had begun shutting down, and around quarter past five the two remaining Levys did the same thing.

Each of them carried a briefcase as they left the booth. They walked out together, and Vito and I followed them. The crowds had thinned out, and most of the booths were already closed. The floor was littered with flyers and crumpled paper cups and the air smelled of spilled coffee and stale pastry.

The brothers stopped at the curb, under the overhang, and it looked like they were having an argument. Moises turned to walk away, and Baruch took his shoulder. They argued again, and Vito and I were about to walk up to them and see what was going on when Ricardo approached them from the direction of the garage on Seventeenth Street.

Vito turned to me. "Ricardo will recognize you. So you stay on Baruch, and I'll follow Moises and Ricardo and see where they're going."

Moises split off from his brother and went up to Ricardo. They shook hands and spoke for a moment, and then Ricardo led Moises back the way he had come from.

Baruch stood there watching them leave for a moment. He shook his head. Then he turned away from them and started across the street toward the parking lot.

Vito followed Ricardo and Moises. I hung back, watching Baruch go through the crosswalk and step into the parking lot. As he did, a big black Hummer pulled out of a parking space and started toward him. I thought for a minute the car was going to hit him—but instead, a big guy in a black T-shirt and jeans jumped out of the car and reached for the briefcase.

I grabbed my cell phone and pressed the speed-dial for Vito, and as I did I ran toward Baruch. He began yelling and fighting off the big guy from the Hummer. "FBI!" I yelled, holding out my badge with one hand, the phone with the other.

"What's going on, rookie?" Vito asked. "Motherfucker. Is that car going after Levy?"

I didn't answer him. I shoved the phone in my pocket and drew my gun as I got close to the Hummer. "Let him go!" I yelled.

Another guy jumped out of the front seat of the Hummer and drew a gun on me. I was so nervous I was shaking, but I did my best to take a deep breath and pull the trigger, aiming for body mass.

Out of the corner of my eye I saw Vito barreling toward us. I just kept moving forward, shooting at the guy with the gun. Around me I heard people screaming, heard a siren and saw flashing blue lights.

I remembered what Vito had said to me, at the warehouse raid, that he always reminded himself that the next op was the one that would kill him. Was this the next one for me? Vi Cunha appeared over the top of the Hummer from the driver's side with a rifle aimed at me.

I'm right-handed, so I had my right hand on the trigger, with my left hand wrapped around the right. I began firing at her, once again aiming at center mass. I had just shot the last of the fifteen rounds from my Glock .22 when I saw her topple backwards and the rifle clatter down with her.

At the same time as I watched her fall, I felt like someone punched me in the chest, really hard, and I fell back on my ass on the pavement. It scared the shit out of me, because it took my breath away, and it took me at least thirty seconds to realize that I'd taken the impact of a bullet in my vest.

Vi's collapse took the steam out of the rest of the

team, and the two other guys threw down their weapons and held up their hands. Miami Beach cops converged on the scene, shouting at the bad guys, and Vito headed in my direction. Baruch staggered toward both of us, still clutching his briefcase.

It was hard to focus with all the noise around us—sirens, people yelling, even a news helicopter overhead. I took a couple of deep breaths and looked up.

"You all right, rookie?" Vito asked, leaning down toward me.

I nodded. "Yeah," I said. "It'll be the next one that kills me."

25
KILLER TEAM

Vito laughed and stood back up, as a couple of EMTs hurried over with a rolling stretcher. Vito helped me stand, and one of the EMTs got me out of my suit jacket and onto the stretcher. It was blazing hot, and sweat poured off my forehead and dripped under my arms.

Vito turned to Baruch. "You did well, Mr. Levy. You held onto that briefcase."

Baruch nodded. "Over a million dollars in here." He lifted up the case and punched in a code, and the lid popped open.

The case was empty.

A string of what I assumed were Spanish curse words spilled out of his mouth. The red and blue flashing lights in the background strobed over his face.

"You didn't know that your brother switched cases with you?" I asked Baruch, swiping a hand over my forehead.

He shook his head. He looked like he was in shock.

"What were you guys arguing about?" Vito asked.

"He wanted to go with his friend, and I said we had to go back to the hotel together. But I never dreamed he was going to run off with the diamonds."

"You think that's what he did?" Vito continued. "He ran off with his friend and your merchandise?" When Baruch nodded again, he asked, "Any idea where he was going?"

"No. I cannot believe he would do this to us, to his family." He put his hand on Vito's sleeve. "You have to find him. My firm is ruined without those diamonds. We have insurance, but there are exceptions if one of us is involved in a theft."

I started to ask if Baruch knew about his brother's relationship with Ricardo, but a pain from my chest zinged through me and I couldn't speak for a moment.

"You go to the hospital," Vito said, pushing against me with his elbow. "I'll take it from here."

"The bullet didn't even hit me," I said. "I'll be fine."

"You still need to get looked at. Take him away," Vito said to the EMTs.

I didn't want to get on the stretcher, but one EMT pushed me down and the other started rolling me away.

"Vito!" I called. I tried to tell him to ask Baruch about Ricardo, but another shock of pain hit me, and I coughed instead.

"You did good, rookie," he said. "Now get the fuck out of here."

The EMTs wouldn't even let me use my cell phone in the ambulance. At the hospital, they made me take off my vest, my shirt, and my T-shirt, took my blood pressure and my pulse, kept fussing with me. My chest hurt when I took deep breaths, but I tried not to let it show. I just wanted to get out of there and get back to work.

I had to have a series of X-rays—hold my arms above my chest, hold my breath, turn sideways—it all seemed like such a waste of time. Then I had to wait forever for someone to tell me the results. Finally, a young Indian doctor with a lavender turban and stickpins in his beard came in to see me.

"You were very lucky, Mr. Green," he said, when he was finished listening to my chest. "You only have one fractured rib."

"What does that mean?"

"Your ribs serve two purposes. They protect the organs in your chest, and they help you breathe by keeping space open in your chest while the muscles you use to breathe contract. These muscles pull on the ribs—so when you fracture one of them, you will experience pain when breathing."

"Already having that," I said. "How long does it last?"

"It can take up to six weeks. To speed things up, you can put ice packs on your chest, get extra rest, and take aspirin for the pain. Lie on your injured side, and be sure to cough or take the deepest breath you can at least once an hour."

"That's all? You don't have to wrap it up or anything?"

He shook his head. "We used to do that. But now we feel it increases the risk of pneumonia or lung collapse."

"So I don't have to stay here? I can go home?"

"As soon as we get your records completed."

He left, and Vito stepped in, exhaustion evident on his face and in his posture. "Hey, rookie, how you doing? You look like shit."

I took a deep breath, and winced. I used my open hand to indicate my hospital gown. "You like my new fashion statement? I'm thinking of wearing it next time I go to Lazy Dick's."

Vito laughed. "You got balls, Angus, going after those guys by yourself. I saw you as I was running up. Classic form."

"But I still got shot."

"Happens to the best of us. At least you young bucks heal damned fast. Though I got to tell you, the Bureau prefers it when we don't get shot. Too much paperwork."

"What happens now?"

"Ricardo and Moises have gone to ground. Moises's rental car was still in the convention center lot, and we've got an APB out on Ricardo's SUV. Baruch and Jacobo are hopping mad. Neither of them had a clue that their little brother was gay."

"Sounds like I'm missing all the fun."

"There'll still be FD302s for you to work on when you get back," Vito said. He yawned. "Listen, I've got to get some shut-eye. Catch you on the flip side."

"Hold on, Vito. Who was in the SUV? That was Vi Cunha, wasn't it?"

He nodded. "She's in surgery right now, but we talked to the guys with her. It was supposed to be a snatch and grab— Ricardo arranged for Jacobo to get sick, and told his cousin that Baruch would have the diamonds. She promised to cut him in for a percentage of whatever she made."

"So Ricardo and Moises double-crossed her and the other brothers?"

"That's what it looks like."

I tried to think through the situation, but I was drowsy and I nodded off. When I heard the curtain open the next time and looked up, I expected to see the doctor, but instead it was the SAC.

"Good work today, Angus," he said.

"Thank you, sir. Did I… did she…?"

"Violeta Cunha survived the surgery she had to remove the bullet you fired into her neck," he said. "She'll live to stand trial."

"That's good," I said.

"Yes, it is. How are you feeling?"

"Tired. It hurts a little when I breathe. But the doctor says all I need is some rest."

"Take a couple of days, then. Rest."

"Thank you, sir."

"Thank you, Angus. You served the Bureau and your country today. I appreciate it."

He left, and the nurse came in and said I was good to go. I pulled on my T-shirt, then found the hole where the bullet had penetrated my shirt and stuck my finger through it. The shirt would make a good souvenir. I slipped it on and buttoned it up. Then I picked up the Kevlar vest and found the bullet embedded in it. I'd have to turn the vest in and get a new one. I wondered if they'd let me keep the bullet.

I folded up my tie and put it in my jacket pocket, slung my jacket over my shoulder, and walked out to the checkout counter. My chest still hurt, but I felt pretty damn good.

After I was finished there, I took a cab back to the lot where I had left my car. It was nearly deserted, the show long since ended. They'd even hosed down the lot so I couldn't tell where the blood had been spilled.

I drove home, took a couple of aspirin, and went right to sleep. By the time I woke Friday morning Jonas was long since gone for work. Getting out of bed, I was reminded of the pain in my chest. I took more aspirin, and practiced those deep breaths.

I forced myself to gather up all my dirty laundry, grumbling about the pain in my chest every time I bent over. While searching through the pockets I found a business card that read Thomas Laughlin in an elegant script, with an address on North Ocean Drive in Fort Lauderdale, a phone number, and an e-mail address. I almost tossed it, but something about its simplicity intrigued me. Who gave out cards without a business name or title?

The card stock was too expensive, the style too old-fashioned, to belong to an unemployed kid. I closed my eyes and held the card in my hand, as if I could call up some psychic vibe to remember the man who'd given it to me. Thomas. Tom.

Oh. Tom. The silver fox at Lazy Dick's. I had bought him a vodka tonic, and he had told me where to find that pain clinic. He also mentioned that Ricardo sometimes used his neighbor's townhouse when his neighbor wasn't home. Was it possible that Ricardo and Moises had gone to ground there? I had to get to Tom quickly; if he knew where Ricardo was, the Bureau needed that information ASAP. Intelligence was like milk, after all.

I dialed the number on the card. When he answered, I said, "Tom? It's Angus Green. We talked at Lazy Dick's the other day."

"Of course. I never forget a handsome face."

"I ended up with the day off at the last minute, and I was hoping we could meet up for coffee this afternoon. I have some more questions for you, and at the same time,

I'd like to hear more about your background and maybe get some mentoring advice from you."

"I'm afraid you caught me on my way out the door. I've got a bit of consulting work that's going to take up most of the afternoon. How about if you let me buy you dinner tonight instead?"

"Oh, you don't have to do that."

And I didn't want to wait that long, either. But if Ricardo and Moises were at his neighbor's townhouse, they were likely lying low for a few days. They had to know we'd be on the lookout for Ricardo's SUV, and that we'd have alerted the airports and cruise terminals.

"No strings attached, Angus. I'm not trying to romance you. I just enjoy dining out but hate to do so alone. A handsome, intelligent young man without designs on my wallet or similar ulterior motives would be a delightful companion."

I winced. I did have an ulterior motive, but at least it wouldn't cost Tom more than dinner. "You do know how to flatter a boy. I'd be delighted to have dinner with you."

We agreed to meet at seven at a seafood restaurant at the Galleria shopping center, a mile inland from the ocean. Even though he'd said it wasn't a date, I felt guilty about going out with Tom when I hadn't seen or spoken to Lester all week. If he'd worked the late shift at the Equinox, though, it was too early to call him. I settled for a text.

I was supposed to stay in bed so that my cracked rib could heal, but I was too restless to take a nap. I settled for bringing my laptop to bed with me, and logged into my Bureau e-mail. I read through all my messages and alerts, and then got up to transfer my laundry from the washer to the dryer. I was halfway through when my cell rang. I scrambled back to my room to grab it, hoping it was someone from the Bureau calling me back in to work.

It was Lester, which was almost as good. "Dude," he said. "You give up on Equinox so fast?"

"Maybe on Equinox, but not on you," I said, walking back to the niche by the garage where the washer and dryer were. "Had to work late all week. Then I got shot."

"Shot? How? I thought you were just an accountant."

I cradled the phone on my shoulder and shoveled the laundry into the dryer, my chest whanging with pain. I told Lester the story. "I'm afraid I'm going to be out of commission for a few days," I said. "Strictly bed rest."

"Cracked ribs are a pain," he said. "I've had a few of them. 'S all right, I guess. I'm working all weekend anyway."

"Next weekend, then." I hung up and went back to my laptop, searching the news sites to see what they were saying about the convention center robbery attempt. There was almost nothing anywhere, and I wondered if it was being covered up, or if the information just hadn't filtered down yet.

An hour later, I was hanging up my shirts when Elton John began singing from my cell phone. I grabbed for it. "Danny? Are you okay?"

"I'm such a fuckup, Angus." He sniffled. "I'm at the police station in State College. This is my one phone call."

"Holy shit, Danny. What's going on?"

"I kept looking around for that skimmer thing you told me about, and I found it stowed away at the back of a cabinet at La Scuola. I had it in my pocket when that detective came back to the restaurant, and he caught me with it."

He was full on crying by then. "Angus, what am I going to do?"

"Listen to me, Danny." I gave him a moment to stop crying. "If you didn't steal any credit card numbers, the police will figure that out. All they have to do is look around your dorm room and check your bank account and they'll see that the only money there is what I transferred to you."

"About that," Danny said.

I groaned. "Don't tell me. You've been spending that money, haven't you?"

"Not all of it."

I closed my eyes and took a couple of deep breaths. Now was not the time to lash out at Danny for being irresponsible, even though I wanted to fly up to Pennsylvania to knock some sense into my brother. I took a deep breath. "Don't worry about that now. What's important is that you tell the truth to the police. Make sure to tell them you think Rocket was the one using the skimmer."

"I did. But I don't think they believe me."

"Give me the detective's name. I'll call him myself." I twisted around to look for a pen and paper, and a spasm of pain hit me so hard I moaned out loud.

"Angus? Are you okay?"

"I got shot yesterday. But I'm fine, really."

His voice went up an octave. "You got shot?"

I gave him the abbreviated version of the story, which was too complicated to get into in great detail anyway. "I don't know what got into me," I said. "I wasn't thinking, just acting on instinct."

"Did you kill anybody?"

"Not for lack of trying. I emptied the magazine in

my gun. But it's a lot harder to hit somebody while you're running toward them."

"Wow." He sighed deeply. "All this shit, it makes me recognize the people around me who matter. Like you, bro. I've only got one brother, and I need him around for a long time. So you better take care of yourself, all right?"

"Will do, Danny."

I sat up, and tendrils of pain shot through my chest. But lying around pampering myself was not part of my agenda. I called the police detective in State College and left him a message. Then I had to get ready to meet Tom for dinner, where I was going to learn everything he knew about Ricardo Lopez and where he might be hiding out. And if there was even a chance that he and Moises might be shacked up next door to Tom, I'd be right on the phone to Roly and Vito.

26
PROPOSITION

Jonas got home as I was getting ready to meet Tom for dinner. I was relieved to be out of my FBI drag, so for dinner I had chosen a pair of comfortable shorts and an oversized polo shirt that could hide my gun.

"Where are you off to?" he asked. He was wearing his own version of work drag: polyester slacks, a light blue shirt, and a cheap tie he'd bought at the flea market for five bucks. He needed a haircut and a shave.

"Place called Truluck's," I said. "At the Galleria."

"Wow. You get a raise or something?"

"Nah. I'm meeting this guy who wants to buy me dinner."

He flopped on the sofa. "Dish."

I looked at my watch. I still had time to make it to my dinner reservation, and I realized I hadn't told Jonas about getting shot. I sat down across from him, careful of my injured rib, and started to run through everything.

"Hold on," he said, when I got to the part about Ricardo

running off with Moises Levy. "You mean that skank had a rich sugar daddy all along?"

"Not a daddy. The guy was only early thirties. Like Ricardo's age." That made me stop and think. "You know where Ricardo was from?"

Jonas shrugged. "Mexico?"

"Yeah, but where in Mexico?"

Jonas pursed his lips, which meant he was thinking. "Maybe Mexico City? He told me once that he grew up in this neighborhood named for a countess. Then he kind of vogued like he was a countess, too." He struck a pose.

A countess. That sounded familiar. All three Levy brothers lived in the same neighborhood in Mexico City. "Could it be Condesa?" I asked.

"Sounds like it. Why is that important?"

"May not be," I said. But my mind was racing ahead. I had assumed that Ricardo had known Moises back in Mexico City because he'd given Ricardo the bracelet. But what if their relationship went even farther back? To before Moises was married? I found it hard to imagine Moises giving up his family and his business for a casual trick, but what if they had been lovers for a long, long time, and this was their one chance to be together?

"So go back," Jonas said. "You're following these jewelers, and suddenly Ricardo shows up and goes off with one of the brothers."

I went through the attempt to steal the briefcase from Baruch, and the revelation that it was empty, and the discovery that Moises had managed to swap the cases without his brother's knowledge. "Then after I got out of the hospital I came home and crashed."

"Excuse me? The hospital?"

"I told you. The bad guys were shooting right and left. I got shot, but the vest stopped the bullet. I just ended up with a cracked rib."

"Angus, Angus, Angus. You got shot? You didn't even wake me up when you got home."

"It's no big deal, Jonas. I'm just supposed to take a couple of days off and rest. But it's hard to do that; you know me. Which is why I called this guy I met at Lazy Dick's to have dinner."

"You called a guy and invited him to dinner at Truluck's? Do you know how expensive that place is?"

"He picked it, and he offered to treat," I said, hating the defensive tone in my voice. The truth was I had no idea the place was expensive. It was at the mall. I figured it was an average sort of restaurant. "Crap. He told me it wasn't romantic."

"Who is this guy, anyway?"

"His name is Tom Laughlin. Older guy, kind of a silver fox."

"Must be one of the wilted flowers who hangs around the bar. But he's got to have bucks to take you to Truluck's. And dude—you can't go there in shorts. You've got to dress it up."

"Oh, fuck. I just wanted to chill."

I stood up, my chest aching, and went back to my bedroom. I resisted wearing a suit, but I did have a nice navy blazer and neatly pressed khaki slacks. A light-blue oxford cloth button-down shirt completed the picture.

When I got to the restaurant I was glad I'd taken Jonas's

advice. It was very elegant—dim lighting, thick carpets, and a bow-tied maître d' who knew Tom by name.

Tom looked very good himself. A single-breasted black sports jacket in what looked like silk, with a light green polo shirt underneath. A simple gold chain around his neck, a gold watch and a matching bracelet around his wrist. Class all the way.

"I'm so glad you called me," Tom said, when we were seated, heavy menus in hand. "Your generation's experiences are so different from mine, and I'm fascinated by the comparisons."

"We couldn't be where we are without the struggles that men of previous generations went through," I said.

I let him guide my choices because I was uncomfortable with the prices, and because I didn't have a lot of experience with fine dining. I ended up with Caesar salad and filet mignon, and we split side dishes of hash browns and sautéed mushrooms.

From the way Tom leaned toward me and his eyes glittered in the light, I could tell that he wanted to talk. So instead of jumping right in and asking about Ricardo Lopez, I sat back to listen.

He began to speak about what it had been like for him as a closeted gay man in the 1960s and '70s. "They were very difficult times," he said. "My family was Irish Catholic, in Boston, and the Church was very clear that homosexuality was deviant. If I revealed myself in any way I'd be ostracized from my family and my community. I wouldn't be able to find a job, and without a job I couldn't afford a home."

"That's terrible."

The waiter soundlessly delivered our salads. "I knew

other gay men, of course," Tom continued, when the man had gone. "We had our signals and our meeting places. None of us were virgins." He smiled. "But so many were fragile souls who couldn't cope. There was a lot of alcoholism and drug abuse. Suicide. Several of my friends and I had what we called closet pacts."

"What were those?"

"We traded keys to each other's apartments. If anything happened to one of us, the other was to immediately go over and empty the closet of porn and sex toys, so his family would never know."

It was an awfully sad idea, but at least these men had the support of friends. I tried to find some comfort in that, but it was hard.

We ate as we spoke, and then the salad plates were replaced with our entrées. "They were desperate times," Tom said. "And then of course AIDS struck, and many men who had been keeping secrets couldn't do so any longer. There was an awful lot of anger and heartbreak. Women who had no idea their husbands were *that way* discovered not only that they were married to faggots, but that they had contracted a fatal disease."

There was a great deal of bitterness in his voice, and I wondered just how much he had been affected, but I didn't know him well enough to pry. "I'm so glad things are different now," I said.

He shook his head. "Don't be so sure. There's still a lot of homophobia in the world, particularly in the Latin and African-American communities. The term 'the down low' may have gone out of fashion, but I guarantee you there are a lot of men still living that lie. And I'm sure they are going through the same pain my generation went through."

He finished his filet and pushed the plate aside. "But I've been monopolizing the conversation. I want to hear more about the kind of work you do. How does an accountant come to work for the FBI?"

I took a deep breath. I'd have a chance soon to ask Tom about Ricardo, but I'd get a better result if the topic came up organically in our conversation.

"A lot of what the Bureau does today requires the skills of accountants and attorneys," I said, spearing the last piece of my steak, which had been cooked perfectly. "Honestly, I spend most of my time with spreadsheets and databases."

"So your being gay has no effect whatsoever on your job?"

"I can't say that. Most of the time, I don't consider myself different from any of the other agents. But I know who else in my office is gay, and every time somebody asks if I'm married, or what I did over the weekend, I have to stop and think about what I want to say."

He nodded. "In my last days at the bank, I was beginning to take some tentative steps out of the closet. It was interesting to see how some people changed their attitude toward me—a few for the better, a few for the worse."

"Did you happen to see the strip trivia contest at Lazy Dick's?" I asked.

"I wouldn't have missed it. You were a great champion."

I blushed as the waiter arrived to remove our dinner dishes. "Why don't you try the chocolate malt cake," Tom suggested. "And if I may, I'll steal a sliver. My trainer won't begrudge me that much—but a whole piece of my own?"

He shook his head. "The man's brutal, but he keeps me in shape."

We both ordered decaf cappuccinos, and when the waiter was gone, I continued. "I didn't realize it at the time, but two of my colleagues from the Bureau were in the audience for the contest. They were there to meet an informant who never showed up. Because they felt I had an inside track at the bar, they brought me onto their task force, and I ended up with my first real field assignment."

"Congratulations! I assume that's the case that brought us into contact."

"It is. Unfortunately it didn't work out the way I had hoped."

"Ricardo wasn't able to help you?"

"Ricardo is right in the middle of the case," I said. "But he disappeared yesterday afternoon and hasn't been seen since."

"Maybe you haven't seen him," Tom said. "But I have. He's living in the townhouse next door to mine."

My adrenaline soared. I knew it! But I tried to stay calm. "Really? How do you know?"

"I saw him coming back from the convenience store with a quart of milk and a box of donuts as I was returning from my run this morning." He smiled. "I felt very virtuous."

"You're sure it was him?"

He nodded. "I have a lot of opportunities to observe the young men at Lazy Dick's," he said. "Ricardo has a distinctive tattoo of an Aztec head on his left ankle. And as I might have told you, he has a habit of using my neighbor's townhouse when my neighbor is not there."

I remembered seeing that same tattoo on Ricardo's ankle

when he was having sex in the men's room at Equinox. Holy crap. I'd just found out where Ricardo and Moises were.

"Would you excuse me for a moment?" I asked, squirming out of the booth. I hit my rib on the edge of the table and pain zoomed through my chest but I gritted my teeth. I walked out of the restaurant and out to the edge of Sunrise Boulevard, away from the valet parkers and patrons waiting for the return of their cars.

I dialed Vito's cell.

"What is it, rookie? I'm having dinner with my wife, and you're supposed to be resting."

"I think I know where Ricardo Lopez is hiding out."

"Jesus Christ!" I heard him apologizing to his wife, and he told me to hold on. A moment later he said, "All right. What do you know?"

I told him quickly about meeting Tom at Lazy Dick's, and having dinner with him, mentioning that Ricardo was missing, and his knowledge of Ricardo's tattoo. I read him the address from Tom's business card.

"Good intel, rookie. Now here's what you do," Vito said. "You get the exact address of the house where he thinks Lopez is and you text it to me. You warn him not to engage the guy at all. Then you go home."

My adrenaline soared even higher. It was my case, and I didn't want to be shut out of it. "But Vito. I'm fine, really. I can get in where you guys can't. I can go home with this guy Tom, be right there on the inside."

"This is not from me, rookie. Didn't the SAC tell you to take some time?"

"And I did. I took today."

"Nothing's going to happen for a while. We're going to

track the ownership of the townhouse. We're going to stake it out and establish who's there. It's gonna be a day or two before we move. I'll call you, all right?"

"Thanks, Vito."

I hung up and went back into the restaurant. I slid back into the booth just as my dessert and our coffees arrived. "I passed on what you told me," I said. I wanted to be honest with Tom—but at the same time I was determined not to get shut out of the case that I had come to think of as my own. I didn't care what Vito said, and though the SAC had indeed told me to take some time and rest, he hadn't said I couldn't keep working the case.

But I didn't want Tom to get the wrong idea, because that would only hurt him. I phrased my words carefully. "The Bureau is going to need more verification. Can I come back to your house with you and see for myself?"

27

STAKEOUT

"If that's your fumbling attempt at a proposition, Angus, I have to tell you it's not that appealing. And I did say I didn't expect any romantic complications from this evening."

"It's not a proposition. I need your help." I explained that I was sure I was going to be shut out of the case. "I won't do anything to put you in danger," I said. "I'm sure they won't let me do anything, anyway. I just want to be there when it happens, and if I'm at your place at least I can see it go down."

I clenched my hands together. "Please, Tom? I won't be any trouble, I promise. I'll sleep on the couch, or on the floor. I'll clean up after myself in the bathroom."

Tom picked up his fork. "You promised me just a sliver of your cake," he said. I turned the plate toward him and he cut a slim slice, which he transferred to the extra plate the waiter had delivered.

I stirred my cappuccino with a stick of rock crystal as

Tom cut the tiniest bite of cake and lifted it to his mouth. He tasted it, then sighed with pleasure. "Delicious," he said.

My chances at staying involved in the case were slipping away, but I didn't think continuing to beg would convince Tom. I forced myself to hold back. I sipped the cappuccino, then tasted the cake. "You're right, this is great," I said.

Tom nibbled at his bit of cake and drank his coffee, and I ate and drank as well. "I've taken too few chances in my life," he said eventually. "With my career as well as my love life. I might as well have a little adventure now. But we'll have to be sensible about this."

"Sensible how?"

"My only guest parking is the single space in front of my townhouse. Your cute little car is quite noticeable. I suggest that I follow you back to wherever you live. You can pick up your necessities, and then I'll drive you to my house. I'll pull into my garage, and then we'll be tucked in as tidily as Ricardo and his lover are in their house."

It was an interesting choice of words. Men of his generation used the term "lover" where men of mine said boyfriend or partner. "That would be great," I said.

The waiter offered Tom the check in a black leatherette case. Tom handed him a credit card without even looking at the bill, and the waiter faded away. He was back a moment or two later, and Tom did a quick mental calculation, added the tip, and signed the check.

"Thank you for dinner," I said. "It was delicious. And I really enjoyed our conversation."

Tom looked at me, and there was a bit of a twinkle in his eye. "Yes, right up to the point when I provided you with the information you came looking for," he said. "But don't worry, I enjoyed our evening as well."

Tom had left his BMW with the valet, while my Mini Cooper was in the garage. We agreed to meet at the back of the mall, and I led him to my house. I was glad to see that Jonas's car was gone; I hoped he was off on a date with Billy the bear. "Sorry about the mess," I said to Tom as I unlocked the front door.

"It's not *Better Homes and Gardens*, but it has a certain frat-boy charm," Tom said dryly.

Seen through his eyes, the place was a dump. I rented my room from Jonas, who leased the house from a guy who had inherited it from his grandfather. The fifties-style furniture was old and worn, the carpeting threadbare. The house had good bones, and I could see it would be an excellent fixer-upper. Neither Jonas nor I were interested in that, though.

"I'll just be a minute," I said, leaving Tom in the living room. I hurried into my bedroom and tossed some clothes into a suitcase. I didn't think I'd be staying with Tom long, but I wasn't sure if I'd need my FBI drag, or more casual wear. I'd be embarrassed to wear anything torn or tattered in front of Tom, which narrowed my choices.

Then into the bathroom to gather my toiletries. When I returned to the living room Tom was admiring a black-and-white Tom Bianchi photo of young nude guys romping around a swimming pool. "I like your taste in art," he said.

I was embarrassed to admit that it belonged to Jonas, but I did. "I haven't had time to do much decorating," I said. "The truth is that I don't have that decorating gene." I motioned around the room. "Jonas doesn't seem to have it either."

"You're a hard-working young man on a limited budget," Tom said. "Give yourself time to develop your own taste, and your wallet."

"And you're very kind," I said. "Ready to go?"

We headed east on Sunrise Boulevard, back past the Galleria, now closing down for the night, and then turned north on A1A. The ocean was dark except for the lights of a container ship already far out to sea.

"This really is very nice of you," I said. "I know it's incredibly rude of me to impose."

"It is ballsy," he said with a smile. "But I like that about you, Angus. You're a very determined young man. And as I said, I ignored too many opportunities when I was a young man. I made a pledge when I came out of the closet that I wouldn't do that anymore."

We passed the dark, shadowy bulk of Hugh Taylor Birch state park on our left. A few cars remained in the parking spots along the beach, but the sidewalk was deserted. We came to the section of beach that a bad winter storm had eroded, and A1A narrowed to two lanes as we passed a long line of million-dollar single-family homes with ocean-facing views.

"Not too far now," Tom said. "Up ahead on the left." He pointed to a row of eight townhomes sandwiched between high-rises. We passed them, then made a U-turn across the median. He signaled and then turned into the third driveway from the end, pressing a remote to open the garage.

The BMW slid easily inside, leaving room on both sides. "Home sweet home," Tom said, as he pressed the remote to close the door behind us. We stepped out of the car, and he pointed to the right. "Ricardo and his lover are on that side. If you noticed, that garage backs up against mine."

I grabbed my bag and followed him inside. "Let me explain the layout," he said. "The townhouses are all the same, though every other one is a mirror image of its neighbor."

He motioned to a low table by the entrance. "You can put your bag there while I give you the twenty-five cent tour."

The claw-foot mahogany table looked like a priceless antique, but I did as he said, placing my duffle there very gently.

He stood in the entryway and motioned left. "You've already seen the garage. To your right is the courtyard." I glanced through sliding glass doors to see pink, red, and yellow hibiscus plants in large clay pots lining stucco walls beneath wire-frame sculptures of birds in flight. Two lounge chairs sat beside an umbrella-topped table.

"As you can see, the courtyard is very private," Tom said. The wall separating it from the street was at least eight feet tall.

"Ahead of us is the living room, to the left the breakfast nook and the kitchen." He walked forward, and I followed. His living room was the kind I wished I had—with comfortable leather couches and a large TV set in a dark wood armoire. A few tasteful knickknacks on shelves. Nothing fussy.

A French baker's rack lined with oversized art books stood against the wall in front of us. "Now you can get your bag, and I'll show you the guest room."

I picked up my suitcase and followed him through the open door beside the baker's rack. "I keep this room very simple," he said. "I believe that guests, like fish, begin to stink after three days, so I don't want to encourage any of my New England connections to take up residence down here for too long."

The guest room looked pretty nice to me. A double bed with an Amish-style quilt, a dresser and desk that were one step up in quality from IKEA, and large landscape photographs that looked like he might have taken them himself. "Bathroom's through there," he said, pointing.

I dropped my bag, and Tom noticed me wince. "You've been having trouble with something all evening," Tom said. "I chose to be polite and ignore it at dinner, but as we're going to be spending some time together, I think you should tell me what's wrong."

My chest really did hurt. "How about if I take some aspirin and meet you back in the living room," I said. "And then full disclosure."

"Fair enough."

I dug the aspirin out of my bag, and found a glass in the bathroom to take them with water. As I did I glanced at myself in the mirror.

Not my best look, I had to say. I was tired, my hair was mussed, and my skin had more than its usual pallor. But I'd be able to sleep soon.

I went back to the living room and found Tom on the sofa. I sat in a hard-backed chair across from him. "I was part of a major operation yesterday afternoon," I said. I gave him a quick rundown of what we'd done, and what my role was. "I got shot. It was nothing serious; my vest took the bullet. But it whammed into me hard enough to crack a rib. That's why I had the day off today. To rest."

"Which it doesn't look like you did," Tom said.

"I did sleep for a while this afternoon. But I guess the whole business took more out of me than I expected."

"Then you should get to bed," Tom said. "We'll talk more in the morning. I'm sure your colleagues can't do anything in the dark anyway, as long as Ricardo and his lover stay tucked up inside."

I had to agree with him. Bureau protocol indicated that agents would stake out the house for a while, either until they spotted Ricardo or Moises, or got a better tip. And Tom was right; the two Mexican lovebirds were probably already in bed.

It took me a while to find a comfortable sleeping position, but once I did, I was out. I woke up with morning wood, confused at first as to where I was. Had I gone home with a trick the night before? That wasn't like me. I looked around the unfamiliar bedroom. It took a moment for the memories to come back.

I picked up my watch. I'd slept for hours, and it was after nine in the morning. My chest still hurt as I stood up, but not as much as it had the day before. I hurried into the bathroom, then pulled on a pair of shorts and a T-shirt and walked out to the kitchen. Tom was sitting at the table, similarly attired, though his shirt was sweaty. He was reading the morning paper and drinking a cup of coffee.

"Good morning, Angus," he said cheerily. "Sleep well?"

"Like a baby." I sniffed the air, and the heavenly aroma of caffeine entered my nostrils. "Any more of that coffee?"

"It's a one-shot cappuccino maker," he said, putting the paper down. "But I'd be happy to make you one. And how about a whole-wheat English muffin to go with it?"

I was careful to hide my frown. "Sounds great," I said.

While Tom busied himself in the kitchen, I picked up the paper. "Page B3," he said over his shoulder.

I flipped there and read about what was called an attempted robbery at the jewelry show, thwarted by the quick action of law enforcement. The Bureau's participation wasn't mentioned, nor was the double-cross engineered by Ricardo and Moises. Ah, the power of a free press.

"When you finish your breakfast, I'll take you upstairs to my bedroom balcony," Tom said. "You'll find at least one of your colleagues parked across the street."

"You've already been out this morning?" I asked.

"I'm not religious about much, but I am about my exercise routine," he said. "Being able to run on the beach every morning makes every penny of this exorbitantly expensive townhouse worthwhile."

"What makes you think there are FBI agents parked across the street?" I asked.

"A portly gentleman in a loud Hawaiian shirt is sitting in a nondescript white car," he said. "I do watch my share of police television programs. And I find it suspicious that he's in his car with the windows rolled up on a beautiful morning like this one." He motioned toward the courtyard, where I could see the sun was shining.

When I finished eating I retrieved my binoculars from my duffle and followed Tom upstairs. His bedroom was very masculine—dark woods, a sleigh bed heaped with striped linens, and framed beach scenes on the walls. He led me across the room to the sliding glass doors, which led to a semi-circular balcony.

Beyond the two lanes of A1A that ran in front of the row of townhouses was the ocean, sparkling blue and green in the morning sunshine. All the on-street parking spots had been taken by early beachgoers. But only one car was occupied, the white sedan Tom had observed.

I zoomed in with the binoculars and saw Vito sitting behind the wheel.

And then I was faced with a dilemma. Did I want to let him know that I was in place? He'd certainly yell at me. But really, what had I done wrong? The SAC had told me to take some time off and rest. I'd done that.

I'd also taken some initiative. I kept going back to my earliest conversation with Roly, when he told me I had unique insight into the case because of my connections with the gay community. Well, I was taking advantage of those.

I pulled out my cell phone and dialed Vito.

"You seen Ricardo yet?" I asked him.

He sighed deeply. "What did I tell you last night, rookie? You stay home and rest up. When I know something I promise I'll call you."

I pulled aside the big glass door and stepped out onto the balcony. I waved at Vito and said, "I'll call you if I see anything, too."

Watching him through the binoculars, I saw that he almost spilled his coffee when he recognized me. But Vito was a true professional, and he caught the cup before it splashed.

28
PLUMBING PROBLEM

"Do you have a problem with following instructions, rookie?" he sputtered. "Because that's gonna kill your career with the Bureau."

"I did what you said, Vito. I went to bed and got some rest. You didn't specify whose bed I had to rest in." I knew I was taunting him, but I had to prove that I was tough enough to play with the big boys.

He spit out a couple of curse words, in English and Italian, and then calmed down enough to say, "All right. Spell it out for me."

"Last night I told you I had a source who put Ricardo in the townhouse," I said. "My source lives next door. I thought it would be a good idea to have an agent in place here, so I asked if I could stay with him. I slept in the guest room last night, and I'm not going to do anything other than stay here and watch and follow your instructions."

He barked out a laugh. "Like I believe that. All right, sit tight. I'll call you back."

I turned back into the bedroom to see Tom leaning against his dresser and smiling. "You're a lot tougher than you look, Angus," he said. "On the outside you're a cute young thing like so many of the boys who hang around Lazy Dick's. Seeing you at the strip trivia contest, I realized you were a lot smarter than most. But between last night and this morning, I'm seeing another side of you."

"I did tell you right at the start that I was an FBI agent," I said.

He laughed. "And that you were an accountant," he said. "Trust me, I've worked with a lot of accountants in my career, and few of them are as ballsy as you are."

"I'll take that as a compliment."

"As well you should. And now that the Bureau knows you're here, shall we sit out on the balcony together and enjoy the sunshine?"

I shook my head. "The Bureau may know that I'm here, but Ricardo doesn't. And I'd like to keep it that way for a while."

He nodded. "Then you'll want to set up inside here. Let me take a shower and get dressed, and then I'll get out of your way."

I doubted Vito would be back to me quickly, so I took a shower as well. I called Jonas and, when he didn't answer, remembered that he was taking a Saturday class. I left him a message that I was fine, staying over with a friend. I thought about calling Lester, but I'd just spoken with him the day before and told him I was going to rest all weekend.

The townhouses adjacent to Tom's had been designed

for privacy, which was unfortunate when you were trying to spy on the neighbors. Tom's windows looked out on the street, his own courtyard, and the blank wall of the townhouse on the other side from the one where Ricardo and Moises were staying.

It was frustrating to be so close and yet have nothing to do. Tom set up a comfortable chair and a small table beside the sliding glass doors that led out to his balcony. The most I could see was the end of the neighbor's driveway, where it reached the street. And the buildings were well-insulated, so I couldn't hear anything through the walls.

Roly called me around ten. "We're sending Wagon in with a device," he said. "Going to look like he's coming from an electronics store."

He disconnected without telling me anything further, and I went to find Tom, who was sitting downstairs in the recliner with a book. "The Bureau's sending a guy," I said. "I don't know why or for what."

I worried that he'd get angry, but instead he said, "Relax, Angus. There are larger forces at work here. When your part becomes clear, you'll play it."

"I wish I had your patience," I said.

"Give yourself some time. It's not something you're born with."

I sure hadn't been. I went back up to my vantage point. Ricardo and Moises were a lot smarter than anyone had given them credit for. They had obviously had this scam planned for a long time. Ricardo had lined up the hidey-hole, and Moises had engineered the three-card monte briefcase swap. If it hadn't been for Paco's phone call, and my noticing Ricardo's bracelet and matching it to the Gustavo Levy logo, they might never have caught the attention of the Bureau, and they could have slipped away. Maybe laid low in Fort Lauderdale for a while, then gone to the house Moises owned in Pennsylvania.

Vi Cunha and Nilady Cruz would have been pissed about the double cross, and so would Moises's brothers, but what was a little family friction compared to a million bucks in precious gems?

About a half hour later, a generic white van I recognized from our motor pool pulled up in the driveway. I went downstairs and opened the door for Wagon.

"Morning, Angus," he said. I stood aside, and he stepped into Tom's house, carrying a square box labeled as if it held a desktop computer. He wore a pair of khakis and a polo shirt with the logo of a popular electronics chain on the breast.

I introduced him to Tom. "Thanks for letting us use your house," Wagon said. "Don't worry, this stuff won't cause any damage."

He sat down on the floor and began unpacking his box. "What is it?" I asked.

"An Eagle sensor," he said, holding up part of the gadget. "It uses low-power, ultra-wideband radio waves to show what's behind walls."

"So we can see if Ricardo and Moises are in there?"

"It's not that precise. The unit can look through walls of up to twenty centimeters of concrete, but it just shows motion of people or animals." He motioned to the wall that separated Tom's townhouse from the one where we believed Ricardo and Moises were hiding. "That's the wall I'm looking through?"

"Yup."

He asked Tom and me to clear a space for him as he assembled a display unit that looked like a handheld video game. Tom and I stood back as Wagon said, "All right. Let's power this baby up and see what we've got."

The unit went through a series of calibrations, and then the display lit up, identifying two sources of heat inside the building. "Their townhouse is the mirror image of this one," Tom said. "That puts them in the kitchen."

Wagon nodded, and then hooked up his laptop to the device and began recording the input information. As we watched, one person stood up and walked around the room, then returned to a seated position.

After Wagon had recorded everything he could from the downstairs, he went upstairs and repeated the process. There were no heat sources up there.

"So looks like two people in the house," Wagon said when we were back downstairs. He had already e-mailed his statistics back to the Bureau. "No guarantee that they're the two you're looking for."

As we watched, both the people in the house next door stood up and moved to the living room. "Doesn't appear that either of them is being restrained," I said. So it wasn't like Ricardo was holding Moises hostage for some reason.

Wagon nodded. "I'll pack up and get out of your way," he said.

After he left, I used the downstairs restroom. Standing before the toilet, I stared at the wall separating Tom's house from its neighbor. I remembered that Tom had mentioned the townhouses were reversed, and had a weird image of Ricardo or Moises standing opposite me, mirroring my own movements.

I washed my hands, and as I tossed the paper guest towel into the trash I noticed an access panel in the wall beneath the sink, which I assumed would allow a plumber to get into the piping behind the wall. I wondered if there was a similar panel on the other side that would lead into the other house.

Too small to crawl through. Despite the many skills my fellow agents had, I didn't know any who were contortionists. But an idea began to form in my head, and I joined Tom in the living room, sitting on the sofa across from him. "You ever have plumbing problems here?" I asked. "Leaks from one house into another, that kind of thing?"

"Not so far. But I've only been here about a year."

"You ever open that access panel in the downstairs bathroom?"

"When the inspector came in to look the place over, before I closed," he said. "If I recall correctly, there's a similar panel in the townhouse next door. But you'd never be able to climb through."

"I wasn't planning to." I told him what I was thinking, and he nodded.

"Feel free to break anything on his side," he said, smiling. "He is harboring a fugitive, after all."

I wondered what was behind the animosity between Tom and his neighbor. Had they both lusted for the same young guy? Or was it as mundane as a noise complaint? Either way, it wasn't my business. "What's your neighbor's name?" I asked.

He gave it to me, and I wrote it down. Then I called Roly. "I have an idea." I explained about the layout of the bathrooms on the first floor. "I don't know much about plumbing, but I wonder if we could get somebody in here to crawl in and cause a leak over there. Then we could have one of the SWAT guys dress up as a plumber and go knock on the front door. Tell them that the next-door neighbor reported to Mr. Parfitt, who owns the unit, that there was a leak in the downstairs bathroom."

"If they're smart, they won't let him in," Roly said.

"Even if they don't, the plumber might be able to get a visual of either Ricardo or Moises to confirm they're in there. And if they do let him in, the plumber can fiddle around for a few minutes, fix whatever we've broken, and give us a visual ID and a sense of what's going on. Maybe even plant a listening device."

"Hmm," Roly said.

"Have a heart, Roly," I said, looking out the window. "Vito's out there sweltering in the heat. If we get somebody inside who says the two guys aren't Levy and Lopez, then Vito can go home."

Roly laughed. "You're a real good Samaritan, Angus. Let me see what I can work out."

29
GOOD NEWS, BAD NEWS

While I waited for the authorization to come through from the Bureau, I asked Tom if he had a screwdriver I could use to remove the access panel. He retrieved a pristine handyman's kit from the garage. A hammer, nails, pliers, wrenches, Phillips and flat-head screwdrivers—everything you could need.

"I'm not very handy," he said. "I usually call someone when anything goes wrong."

"My mom's second husband believes that God helps those who help themselves," I said, carrying the tool kit to the bathroom. "My brother and I had to learn how to do everything around the house."

Tom followed me, standing in the doorway as I settled on the tile floor. "She remarried recently?"

I shook my head. "When I was twelve. But I know what you're going to say. He's not my stepdad. Just her husband."

Tom didn't say anything, just nodded. I cracked open

the tool kit, found the right sized screwdriver, and began removing the screws that held the panel in place. "Flashlight?" I asked Tom.

He returned a moment later with a square hand-cranked one. He began turning the handle. "Hurricane kit," he said, as his strong forearm revved the battery. "You never know when the power's going out. And I'm sure I'd be out of batteries at the wrong time."

The flashlight was cranked up to strength as I removed the panel. Tom handed it to me, and I said, "In case I haven't said so already, I really appreciate your help, Tom. I'm determined to be part of closing this case, and I can't do that without you."

"You're welcome," he said, getting down on the floor next to me. "But get to the action. What can you see?"

He crouched next to me as I shone the light inside, and I got a whiff of what was either his cologne or his bath soap. There wasn't much to see; the false wall between his townhouse and Parfitt's was only about a foot deep and crowded with pipes. My phone buzzed in my pocket, and I had to roll against Tom to retrieve it. The movement had an awkward intimacy I was determined to ignore. I stepped out into the living room to take the call.

"We're in luck," Roly said. "One of our agents grew up with an uncle who was a plumber in Haiti. He thinks he can rig something up. He's on his way to you."

I told Tom, and almost as soon as I hung up my phone rang again. "Hey, Lester," I said.

"How's your rib?" he asked.

"Still hurts. But I got some rest last night."

"Would you like another cappuccino?" Tom called from the kitchen.

"That would be great. Thanks." I turned back to my call. "I thought you were working all weekend."

"That your roommate?" Lester asked.

"Nah, just a friend," I said.

"I didn't think you were the kind of guy who'd jump into somebody else's bed while mine was still warm," Lester said.

I walked toward the guest bedroom. "I don't know what you mean."

"You probably don't remember Mauricio," he said. "One of my buddies from the gym. You met him last Sunday when we worked out."

My brain was filled with case details, and I was having trouble following Lester's train of thought. "Um, maybe," I said.

"He remembered you. And this morning he told me he saw you last night at the restaurant where he works, on a date with some rich guy. After you told me you were going to stay home and rest up."

One of the busboys had looked vaguely familiar, but I'd assumed I recognized him from a bar. "Oh, that," I said.

"And you're with him now, aren't you? You spent the night with him."

"Slow down, Lester." I took a deep breath. "I promise I will tell you the whole story when I see you again. The short version is that I had dinner last night with a very nice older guy named Tom. It wasn't a date; he had some information I needed. I did spend the night at his house—but in his guest room. I'm not sleeping with anyone other than you."

"How can I believe you, Angus? Cops are all the same. You think the regular rules don't apply to you."

I couldn't get angry—I had too much else going on to let my emotions rule. I took a couple of deep breaths and willed my blood pressure to go down. "You're going to have to take this one on faith, Lester," I said. "You've spent enough time with me to know I'm not a skank." I paused. "Staying here last night, being here today, is all tied into my case. I can't tell you how or why right now. But I promise you that once this is over I'll tell you everything. Can you hold off on judging me until then?"

Lester was quiet, and I was afraid for a moment that he'd hung up. "Guys look at me and they see this big bruiser," he said. "But I've got a heart just like everybody else, and I don't want to get it stepped on."

"I know, and I know it's a big heart," I said. "That's why I'm confident you're going to see this is all a big nothing. All right?"

"Call me when you can. I gotta go."

I went back to the kitchen, where Tom was finishing my second cappuccino of the day. "Some things never change," he said, handing me the mug. "Even with how far we've come in bringing our relationships out into the open, we're still men, and we have jealousy and testosterone."

"How do you handle it?" I asked. "I hate drama."

He laughed. "I don't think that's true, Angus. Redheads have fiery personalities—at least that's what they always say, don't they? I'll bet if you and your boyfriend had your situations reversed, you'd be just as quick to get jealous."

I took a deep breath. "Maybe so," I said. "But he's not even my boyfriend. We've just gone out a couple of times."

Tom shook his head. "I'm not the best role model when it comes to relationships, but I can tell you that if he's reacting the way he is, he thinks he's your boyfriend already."

Yikes. "Can't think about that now," I said. "I have a case to work."

An agent named Ferdy Etienne arrived just before one in the afternoon. Instead of the sharp suits I'd always seen him in, he wore a pair of stained, baggy overalls and a T-shirt with a rip in the neck. His bald head gleamed in the sunshine of the courtyard as I introduced him to Tom, who said, "You FBI agents are really a rainbow team, aren't you?"

I thought for a minute he was assuming that Ferdy was gay, but then remembered that so far he had met me and seen Vito outside, and been introduced to a Chinese guy and now a Haitian. "So are the bad guys in Miami," Ferdy said, shaking his hand.

I led Ferdy to the guest bathroom, and tried not to hover too obviously. Ferdy banged a couple of pipes, twisted some screws, and then called for towels. "May get a bit messy here," he said.

Tom brought him a stack of Ralph Lauren bath towels. Ouch. I hoped they didn't get wrecked. But I wouldn't have expected Tom to be a Walmart shopper.

Ferdy stacked the towels along the inside of the false wall on Tom's side, then turned his wrench once. Water began pouring out of a pipe, flowing directly toward Parfitt's side of the wall. Ferdy replaced the access panel on Tom's side and then stood up.

"Now we give the water a few minutes to find its way," he said in his musical accent.

"Can I offer you something to drink?" Tom asked, and

we all agreed on lemonade. I followed Tom to the kitchen while Ferdy called in his report.

"If there's any damage I'll make sure you get compensated," I said.

Tom laughed. "My dear boy, the intrigue involved here is compensation enough."

The three of us sat at the kitchen table to wait for the water to do its business on Parfitt's side. Tom had been to Haiti for vacations, back in the 1980s when the Club Med there was cheap, and he and Ferdy talked about the island.

About two o'clock, Ferdy looked at his watch. "I think enough time has passed," he said. "I'll come back when I've seen what I can next door."

"You know what they look like?" I asked.

"Photos in the case folder." As Ferdy stood I noticed—because I was looking for it—the outline of his gun underneath the overalls. I hoped there would be no reason for him to use it.

Ferdy left, carrying his toolbox, and Tom put his finger to his lips and led me out to the courtyard. From there we could hear Ferdy knocking on Parfitt's door. We heard his side of the conversation as he spoke through the closed door. Whoever he spoke with didn't want to let him in.

"Check the bathroom yourself," Ferdy said. "I wait."

I was so nervous I could have tap-danced. Finally Parfitt's door opened, and someone invited Ferdy in.

Tom and I went back to the downstairs bathroom. With the access panel back in place, we couldn't hear anything other than the sound of running water and a couple of clanks. Then the water stopped.

Back to the courtyard. We waited there until Ferdy came

to the gate and let himself in, and then he followed us inside. "Good news and bad news," Ferdy said. "The good news? Those are the right two guys."

"And the bad?" I asked.

"It looked like they did a quick clean up before they let me in," he said. "I'm not sure what they were hiding, but they missed one thing, on the kitchen table. Maybe they didn't realize I'd recognize what it was."

I waved my hand hurriedly. "Come on, Ferdy, spill. What is it?"

"A block of C-4." He turned to Tom. "A kind of plastic explosive. Looks like there was enough there to blast this whole block into the ocean halfway to Bimini." He nodded toward the front door. "I've got some calls to make. You guys stay put."

Staying put was not something I did easily. While Tom sat in his recliner, I paced around the living room. "They're going to send me home," I said. "I hate this. Getting so close to solving this case and then being pushed aside."

"Sit down, Angus," Tom said. "You're making me nervous."

I sat on the sofa across from him.

"I've supervised a lot of young men and women just as eager and hard-working as you are," he said. "Part of belonging to a team is recognizing that each member has his or her own skills to contribute. In the end, what matters is the result, the accomplishment."

"I know I'm acting like a spoiled brat, and not an FBI agent." I looked up at him. "But it's hard."

"That's why they call it work, Angus," he said.

Ferdy came in the front door. "Mr. Laughlin?" he asked. "The Special Agent in Charge would like to speak with you."

Tom stood up and took the cell phone from Ferdy. I raised my eyebrows at Ferdy, wondering what was going on, but he just shrugged.

I tried to read Tom's body language. Was the SAC yelling at him for letting me drag him into the situation? That wouldn't make sense. The boss should be coming down on me instead. I wanted to jump to Tom's defense, but I held back.

"I'm honored to be able to help out," Tom said. "I have a friend who lives across the street. I can drive over there, and you'll have use of the townhouse and the garage. And then I'll come home when you're finished."

He listened for a moment. "Thank you. I've spent a lot of time with Agent Green lately, and if he's an example of the kind of men and women you have in your office, then I have every confidence you'll manage this operation very well."

Tom handed the phone back to Ferdy, who said, "Yes, boss. I'll get things moving," and then hung up.

I hoped I'd at least be able to go with Tom to his friend's—but I knew in both my heart and my brain that I couldn't ask anything more of anyone. It was time to be a good boy and follow instructions.

"May I have a few minutes to pack up some things I wouldn't want destroyed?" Tom asked Ferdy, in a remarkably calm voice.

"Absolutely, sir. And thank you."

Without saying anything further, Tom walked over to the

stairs and began to climb. "We've got a lot to get organized," Ferdy said to me. "You know if we have Wi-Fi here?"

"I'm not being sent home?"

"Nobody told me," he said. "I assumed you were part of this team."

My adrenaline surged. I was still on the case. Yowza. "I'll get my laptop set up," I said.

30
WHAT BROTHERS KNOW

Tom packed up and came downstairs with two rolling suitcases. I helped him carry them out to the Lexus. "I don't know what to say, Tom," I said as I lifted them into the trunk, wincing with pain because of my cracked rib. "I should never have asked to come back here with you. If I'd known I might be putting you in danger…."

"You'd have done it anyway," Tom said. "I told you, Angus, I've worked with a lot of very ambitious—even ruthless—people in my career. I saw that in you when you first started taking your clothes off at the strip trivia contest. You were determined to win, and you did. Don't ever apologize for who you are."

"I don't want to be the kind of person who sacrifices everyone around him, even if the goals are noble," I said.

Tom leaned over and kissed my cheek, very gently. "You have a good heart, Angus, as well as a brain and fierceness.

As long as you keep those three qualities in balance, you'll be fine. And don't worry about me."

I stood by the door as Tom backed away. He had left me the remote for his garage door, so I closed the door as he reached the street. When I went back inside, Ferdy was already rearranging the furniture. We cleared the rest of the wall next to Parfitt's townhouse and set up a table there. Ferdy had stuck a listening device to the back of an armoire in Parfitt's living room, so while I made coffee, he configured a laptop to begin recording any conversations from the house next door.

A few minutes later, Roly called, and I opened the garage door so he could pull a Bureau SUV inside. Zolin jumped out of the backseat as I stood in the doorway. "You've got a listening post set up?" he asked.

"Right inside the living room," I said.

He nodded and walked past me. Wagon got out the other side and began unloading weapons from the back. I took a couple of rifles from him and headed inside, passing Roly, who was still in the front seat, talking on his cell.

Wagon assembled the armory on the kitchen table. I grabbed the box containing the speaker phone and began to set it up in the dining room. When Roly walked in from the garage, he came over to me. "You did good, Angus," he said.

"I figured you'd be angry that I didn't follow instructions. Vito seems pretty pissed."

"You know Vito. He's 50 percent bluster and 50 percent pussycat. He'll be fine." He nodded toward Zolin, who already had headphones on. "Good thing we have Agent X on our team. He'll be able to understand anything that goes on over there."

"But you speak Spanish, too," I said.

"Castilian," he said. "And Cuban Spanish, and Spanglish. But Mexican's beyond me."

"I thought it was all one language."

He shook his head. "Every one of the Latin countries has its own dialect. It takes a native speaker to get all the nuances—and that's what we need here. Different slang terms mean different things. A word that means 'bus' to a Puerto Rican is a nasty term to a Cuban. Sure, I speak Spanish. My dad was born in Madrid but raised in Havana. He grew up speaking schoolbook Spanish and he made sure I could speak it too. But for the local slang it's always best to get a native."

Vito came in as we were talking. "Sheryl from Chris Potts's team took over for me outside. Just in time, because I gotta piss like a racehorse," he announced. "Where's the john in here?"

I pointed him toward the guest bath. When he was finished, he joined me, Wagon, Ferdy, and Roly at the dining-room table, and patched in the SAC and a couple of other agents at the office through the speakerphone.

"Where do we stand?" the SAC asked.

Roly nodded to me. "Angus?"

"This is Green, sir," I said. "We have a visual confirmation from Ferdy Etienne that the two men in the townhouse next door are Ricardo Lopez and Moises Levy. He planted a listening device there, and Agent X is monitoring their conversation."

"Agent X?"

I looked at Vito, who was laughing. I had no idea how to pronounce Zolin's last name, and with his headphones on he wasn't listening to us. "He means Xochimilco, or whatever his name is," Vito said.

"Oh, right. Zolin," the SAC said. "Go on."

Ferdy explained that he'd seen C-4 in the townhouse, and that based on the scramble he'd witnessed, he was pretty sure there were weapons there as well.

"Do we know what they want?" the SAC asked.

"We haven't made contact," Roly said. "Waiting to get the team assembled."

"Keep me in the loop," the SAC said, and then he logged off.

Roly ended the call and looked around the table. "Options?"

"We could pipe some gas into the townhouse to knock them out," Wagon suggested. "We've got access through the bathroom wall, right?"

"Too risky for an opening salvo," Roly said. "But we'll keep it as a backup plan." He looked at me. "You know these guys, don't you, Angus?"

I shrugged. "I've talked to Ricardo a couple of times. And met Levy with Vito when we spoke with him and his brothers."

"You want to send the rookie in to negotiate?" Vito suggested. "He's had his panties in a twist to stay on this case."

Roly shook his head. "Too dangerous. We don't know what kind of guns they've got in there, and we don't want to tip our hand."

I wasn't sure if I should have been pleased that Vito suggested me, or irritated at the way he phrased his suggestion. Out of the corner of my eye I saw Zolin with his hand up, trying to get our attention. "I think Zolin's got something."

We all turned toward him. He pulled the headphones off and said, "Levy got a text from one of his brothers. If he gives back the diamonds, they won't press charges, and they can all go back to Mexico."

Roly asked, "Who's been liaising with the brothers?"

"I spoke to the older one, Jacobo, yesterday," Vito said. "Told him to sit tight. Never talked about charges with him."

"If Moises gives back the diamonds, and the brothers say that it was just a misunderstanding, does that clear everything up?" I asked.

"Not that easy," Roly said. "There was a robbery; there were guns involved; people got shot. You can't pass that off as a misunderstanding. Vito, get hold of the brothers. See what they're saying." He turned back to Zolin. "You hear anything else?"

"They're arguing," he said. "Lopez and Levy. Lopez says they're in too much trouble already, that they can't just walk away."

"Which is true," Roly said.

"Does it sound like they're going to separate?" I asked.

"Not yet," Zolin said. "Both of them still saying love stuff." He shrugged. "But if it gets worse...." He put his headphones back on.

Vito pushed his chair back. "I'll call the brothers." He went into the guest room with his cell phone and shut the door.

"It's good that they're arguing, right?" I asked. "We could use one against the other."

"You never know in a situation like this," Roly said.

"Could be good for us, could be bad. There's a lot of testosterone over there, mixed with weapons and explosives."

Sounded a lot like the Bureau to me, but I didn't say that.

Vito came out of the guest room. "I've gotta meet with the brothers. They're going batshit crazy. I'll take the SUV and Green and I'll get back here as soon as I can."

I grabbed the garage door remote and followed Vito to the garage. He was muttering the kinds of Italian curses I'd heard from old ladies in Scranton when I was growing up. My favorite was *brutto figlio di puttana bastardo*—ugly son of a bitch bastard. My friend Jimmy's grandmother was crazy, and she was always leaning out the front window yelling that at kids in the street.

I waited until we'd already backed down the driveway and were heading south on A1A to ask, "Where are we going?"

"Back to frigging South Beach," Vito said. "I don't want to give these brothers any clue that we know where Moises is. We'll meet them at their hotel." He looked over at me. "Don't say a frigging word without my telling you to."

"Why are you bringing me, anyway?"

"Because they know you and they know me. We've got to make this seem like business as usual. Finding out their little brother is gay has them freaked, and maybe you can help with that."

Vito drove like a maniac down Sunrise Boulevard, zigzagging past tourists in rented convertibles, blasting his horn at young guys swaggering through intersections like traffic laws didn't apply to them. "Slow down, Vito," I finally said, as he darted through the parking lot of a strip mall to get ahead of some slow-moving traffic. "You'll give yourself a coronary."

He screeched to a halt at the next red light and fumbled in his pocket for a vial of pills. "For my blood pressure," he said as he popped a couple of them.

I could see him taking some deep breaths. By the time we got onto the highway he was a lot calmer. "We need to convince them to back off," Vito said as we merged into the fast lane. "Let us do our jobs."

"It's their brother, though," I said. "I know how I'd feel if my brother were in trouble. I'd want to do everything I could to get him out."

"That's what we're trying to do," he said. "They've just got to cut us enough slack."

I remembered Danny. The police detective from State College hadn't called me back, and I had no idea if my brother was still in custody, if he'd been charged with anything, if he needed bail.

I pulled out my cell phone and dialed Danny's number. The call went right to voice mail, and I left a message. "Danny, it's Angus. Are you still in custody? I'm going to call the police again."

I hung up, and Vito looked over at me. "What's up?"

I explained Danny's situation. "Do you think I can call up the police station and ask if they're holding my brother?"

"Let me ask. Dial the number and then give me the phone."

"This is Special Agent Vito Mastroianni of the Miami Bureau of the FBI," he said. He recited his badge number to whoever had answered. "I'm checking on the status of someone who may be important to one of our investigations. Daniel Green. You have him in custody?"

He turned to me. "She's checking."

Vito zigzagged around a slow-moving van full of Pentecostal church-goers, and then he said, "Uh-huh. No, no problem. We'll take it from here. Thank you for your help."

He handed me back my phone. "Released yesterday evening."

I took a deep breath. At least he was out of police custody. But I still wanted to know what was happening.

When we pulled up at the Loews, Vito badged the valet and told him to keep the car handy, and we walked into the lobby.

The Levy brothers had moved into a two-bedroom suite to wait things out. Up until now we'd only seen the brothers in business suits, so it was a surprise when the middle brother, Baruch, opened the door wearing a Hawaiian shirt. It was covered in neon hula dancers and oversized board shorts in an electric red pattern that hurt the eyes. He wore flip-flops on his feet and looked like he'd just come from a surfboard rental store.

His older brother Jacobo was as pale as a vampire, wearing suit pants and a white shirt, with the cadaverous appearance of an undertaker on vacation. "You have our diamonds?" he demanded.

"Not yet," Vito said. "But we know where your brother is."

Jacobo waved his hand. "My only brother is right here."

Baruch turned to him and muttered something in what sounded like Yiddish. Jacobo frowned and crossed his arms over his chest.

"Please, sit down," Baruch said. "How is Moises?"

A short sofa faced two chairs in front of a floor-to-ceiling window that looked out at Collins Avenue and the art deco buildings of South Beach.

"We've got the house under surveillance," Vito said as he and I sat on the sofa. "We know where they are and what they're planning. Just give us time to work things out."

"These criminals hold Moises?" Baruch asked.

Vito shook his head. "Your brother doesn't appear to be restrained. He's still with the same man he left the convention center with."

I leaned forward. "Did you grow up in the same neighborhood where you live now?" I asked. "Condesa?"

Vito glared at me. Yeah, he had told me not to talk.

Jacobo said, "Yes. Why?"

"Did your brother ever mention a friend named Ricardo?" I asked. "Back when you were kids?"

The brothers looked at each other, and Baruch said, "Yes, he have a friend, but not good boy. Ricardo…." He motioned to his brother, who shook his head.

"Ricardo Lopez?" I asked.

"Maybe." The plush carpeting and upholstered furniture swallowed all the sound in the room, and I heard the *whoop-whoop* of a siren outside on Collins Avenue.

I pulled out my phone and scrolled to a picture of Ricardo. "Would you recognize him?"

I leaned forward to hand the phone to Baruch, and my cracked rib twinged. He looked at the photo of Ricardo and shook his head. Jacobo pulled out a pair of skinny reading glasses and then moved the phone back and forth in front of his face until he got the picture in focus. "Could be," he said, handing the phone back to me. "This is the man?"

I nodded. "We believe that they've been seeing each other for a long time."

Jacobo bristled. "You are making big mistake. Moises is not homosexual."

Baruch did not respond so quickly. "I think maybe Mr. Green is right," he said, finally. "Moises, he did not want to marry, you remember? Papa force him. And now I think about this other boy, this Ricardo. How he and Moises are together a lot until Papa say Moises must go to college in US. You remember Moises cry?"

Jacobo crossed his arms over his chest. "Moises was silly boy who did not know what was good for him."

"Moises know," Baruch said sadly. "It is we who do not know. And now we have much trouble because of it."

I remembered what Tom had said, about how men in many cultures still had to lie about their sexuality. How sad that poor Moises had gotten trapped in the way he had. It didn't excuse the theft, or Paco's death—but it did explain a lot.

Jacobo and Baruch promised not to try and contact Moises again. We made sure they had both our cell phone numbers and then retrieved the SUV from the hotel valet.

"This is fucked up," Vito said, as we navigated the crowded streets of South Beach. It was already late in the afternoon, and tourists were packing up their beach chairs and sunblock, wrapping themselves in towels and walking back to their hotels.

"Do you think that if Ricardo agrees to testify against his cousin and Nilady Cruz, we could get the DA to work a deal?" I asked. "I mean, is there any good way out of this for Ricardo and Moises?"

"I don't know, rookie," Vito said. "If Ricardo killed Paco, then he's facing jail time no matter what. They turn themselves in, that's the best thing. Before anybody else gets hurt."

Vito's cell rang and he put it on speaker. "Yo, Roly," he said.

"More arguments here," he said. "They might be making a move quicker than we thought. How fast can you guys be back?"

Vito swung onto the MacArthur Causeway, heading west toward the setting sun, which glinted off the high-rise towers of downtown Miami ahead of us in golden shards. "Forty-five minutes to an hour," he said.

"Make it on the short side," Roly said. "If these guys get away from us we may never have this good a chance at them again. And we can't go in after them without knowing what kind of firepower they have."

"Will do," Vito said, and he jumped the curb to dart around a car full of elderly women in bright red hats, who stared at us in horror as we passed. I gave them a cheerful wave and then held on to the door handle as Vito accelerated onto the MacArthur Causeway.

31
NEGOTIATIONS

Vito gripped the steering wheel like an Indy 500 driver, and maneuvered the bulky Bureau SUV as if he were on a track, rather than a crowded highway. I was thrilled and scared in equal parts. I couldn't help imagining the headline: *Two FBI Agents Killed in Fiery Crash on I-95*. But Vito knew his stuff, and aside from the adrenaline rush of a close call with an RV with Montana plates that darted into our lane without warning, I survived the drive without significant heart failure.

As we exited the highway onto Sunrise Boulevard again, darkness beginning to fall around us, I remembered what Vito had suggested. "I want to talk to Ricardo and Moises," I said. "They both know who I am. And I understand their situation."

"Not our decision to make, rookie," Vito said. "But it may come down to that. You think you can manage it?"

"I do. I did well in negotiation in the academy. And I've

got a bunch of things in common with them—being gay, having a brother. I can get through to them."

"We'll float it again when we get back to the townhouse," Vito said.

We pulled into the garage, and then walked inside. Zolin was still at the laptop with his headphones on. Roly, Wagon, and Ferdy were at the dining room table. "Any news?" Vito asked.

"They're packing the SUV," Roly said. "Chris Potts is putting together a team to surround the car and apprehend them. But this area is full of people, and we don't want to risk a shootout—or give them a chance to use that C-4. So we're waiting to see what kind of move they make."

"We need to get to them before they leave," I said.

Everyone turned to look at me. "I want to talk to them." I spelled out the reasons I had given Vito in the car.

Roly looked at Vito. "I say we let him try," Vito said.

"How do you want to play it?" Roly asked, turning to me.

"I like the idea of texting rather than calling, so I can customize the message to each of them. Ricardo knows me, but doesn't know I'm an agent. Moises knows I work for the Bureau but he doesn't know that I'm gay or that I've met Ricardo."

"Give it a try," Ferdy said. "Agent X can listen into what they say."

I already had Ricardo's number in my phone, and the brothers had given us Moises's cell number. In my text to Ricardo, I reminded him that I was the guy he'd met at Equinox with Jonas, told him that I was an FBI agent, and that I could help him out. I ended the message with, *Let's talk*, and saved it to my drafts folder.

Then I wrote to Moises. *I'm gay, too, and I understand your situation. I can help you both. Let's talk.* I looked it over once more, then hit send, and then reopened the message to Ricardo and sent that, too.

I hoped I could do what I was promising. Only the district attorney could make deals with suspects, and I was well aware that I was still a raw recruit, with less than a year's experience under my belt. But my gut told me I could do this, and that it was my obligation to put myself on the line to bring this situation to a safe close.

We all clustered around Zolin. "Levy just announced that he got Agent Green's text," he said, after a minute. "He's reading it out loud to Lopez. Lopez says he got a text, too."

I felt like we were all holding our breath, though of course we weren't. "They're arguing," Zolin said. He grimaced and held the earphones away from his head an inch or two. I could hear loud voices in a blur of Spanish.

Then my phone buzzed in my palm with a text from Ricardo. *Where are u?*

I looked at Roly and Vito. "Ricardo wants to know where I am. Do I tell him?"

They both nodded, so I texted back, *Next door can I cm over?*

Zolin popped the headphones on again. "These guys can get loud," he said.

Even without the listening device, I could hear raised voices coming through the wall. I shifted uncomfortably from foot to foot. I hadn't taken any painkillers all day, and my cracked rib was starting to throb.

The two Mexicans argued for a while. Zolin cracked a smile, and I wondered why, until my phone buzzed again.

No shirt, no pants, no gun, the text read.

I repeated the message out loud. "I don't mind," I said, though my heart was going like a cheetah on the plains of Africa.

"You can't do that," Roly said. "Completely against agency protocol. The SAC will never let you walk into a scene without your weapon and your vest."

"I gotta agree with him, rookie," Vito said. "Non-negotiable."

I called Ricardo's cell and tried to explain to him. Zolin had one headphone on and the other off so he could hear both sides of the conversation.

Ricardo got more and more agitated as I tried to explain the Bureau protocol, that I'd never be able to walk over there in my undies. But panicked people do stupid things, and he shouted a couple of Spanish expletives at me and hung up.

I kept on talking, though, as an idea formed in my head. "All right, Ricardo. I'm glad you trust me. I'll be over in a couple of minutes."

Zolin looked over at me, his eyebrows raised, but he didn't say anything to reveal that he knew Ricardo wasn't playing along.

I went into the guest bedroom and shucked my shorts and T-shirt. I pulled on the khakis I'd worn to dinner with Tom and an undershirt. I was hooking the vest when Roly tapped on the door and stepped inside.

"You shouldn't do this, Angus," he said. "I know you're trying to prove yourself to the team—but it's too big a risk."

"Back when this started, you told me I had unique skills

and access to the information in this case because I'm gay,"
I said. "That's a two-way street."

"What do you mean?" he asked, as I buttoned my shirt,
trying to ignore the pain in my chest.

"It means that a responsibility comes with that access," I
said. "That I have to do what I can to protect these people."

"It doesn't work that way, Angus. We have a responsibility
to protect everybody, as far as we can, without regard to
their skin color, their religion, their country of origin, or
their sexual orientation."

"That's the Bureau line." I picked up my Glock, pointed
it toward the ground, and checked that it was loaded. "But if
you were dealing with somebody who only spoke Spanish,
wouldn't you make an extra effort to make sure that person
got fair treatment, because you had the best ability to
understand him?"

Roly crossed his arms over his chest.

"It's the same thing," I said. "Or even more so. For
decades, maybe centuries even, gay people have gotten the
short end of the stick when it comes to law enforcement. I
want to make sure that pattern stops with me."

I grabbed my cell phone and stepped toward him. "Wish
me luck," I said.

I waved to the other agents and strode out the front
door, closing it gently behind me. Then I walked through the
courtyard and out to the driveway.

I was out of visual contact with everyone except Sheryl,
in the surveillance car on the street. I waved to her. The air
was cooling in the darkness, and a breeze had kicked in off
the ocean. Goosebumps rose on my arms as I walked the

short distance past the two back-to-back garages, and then opened the gate into Parfitt's courtyard.

The floor-length vertical blinds were closed, and I was grateful for the privacy. I took a deep breath. I'd better be a damn good negotiator because my butt was quite literally going to be on the line.

I unhooked my holster and rested it with my gun on top of the rolling trash can. Then I began to strip, folding my clothes into a careful pile. By the time I finished, I didn't feel much like an FBI agent, standing in Parfitt's courtyard in a pair of skimpy red-and-blue-striped cotton boxer briefs, which hugged my butt and equipment tightly.

As a matter of fact, I was terrified, both of what could happen with Ricardo and Moises, and of the possible consequences if my colleagues found out I had gone ahead and taken my clothes off against orders. But I had a job to do, and I was going to do it to the best of my ability.

I rang the doorbell and waited.

Moises answered the door, in a light blue Ralph Lauren long-sleeve shirt and pinwale corduroys. He was still wearing his Star of David, his watch, bracelet, and pinky ring—but his wedding ring was gone. He stepped aside to usher me in.

The living room was as different from Tom's as it could have been, all mirrors and hard-edged metal furniture. Ricardo stood ahead of me, a gun in his right hand pointed at me. It would be hard to miss me at such close range.

"You are fucking FBI," he said. "When you talk to me at bar, you are just playing me, huh? You think you are smart guy?"

"Put the gun down, Ricardo," Moises said. "He's here to talk."

I was almost rigid with fear, yet at the same time I recognized the absurdity of the situation. Ricardo and Moises were both fully dressed, and they were looking me up and down like I was a dancer-stripper at a gay club.

"Talk is shit," Ricardo said. "Is no happy ending to this fairy tale."

I took a deep breath, and my rib ached. I said, "You aren't going to shoot me, Ricardo. Because if you do, then the FBI is going to storm in here with guns blazing, and you and Moises are both going to end up dead. And neither of you wants to die."

Moises crossed the room to him. "He's right, *mi amor.* Put the gun down." He gently pushed the barrel of the gun away from me, and my heart rate began to slow.

Ricardo laid the gun on the glass-topped dining table with a clatter that rattled my already edgy nerves. He nodded toward a stiff-backed metal chair, and I sat down, shivering when my bare back touched the cold metal.

Ricardo and Moises sat on the sofa across from me. "How you find us?" Ricardo asked.

I wiped some sweat from my brow and crossed my right leg over my left. It was absurd how uncomfortable I felt being nearly naked in front of them. "Investigative work and dumb luck. It started when Paco Gonzalez called our tip line and told the agent that he'd sold plans to the convention center to someone, and he was worried that he was helping terrorists."

"That *hijo de puta,*" Ricardo said, shaking his head. "I told him to shut up, but he wouldn't listen."

I was glad that Zolin was next door recording this

conversation. If we needed proof of a connection between Ricardo and Paco, we had it.

"Once I figured out that Paco was dead, I went looking for the guy who saw him last. That would be you."

He gripped the gun on the table with his right hand, but didn't raise it. If he wanted to, he could get at least one good shot at me before I could tackle him.

"All I do is convince him to get in SUV with my cousin and me. She drop me off at my place, then drive him to talk. I don't know where they go or what she say."

Yeah, sure. "So you didn't kill him?"

"No! It was Violeta. After she come back home she yell at me, tell me how stupid I am to trust idiot like Paco."

It was a good story, but it wasn't up to me to believe it or not.

"We knew there was some kind of theft planned for the jewelry show but we didn't know how it was going to happen." I held my arm up and tapped my wrist. "Until I saw your bracelet. That was the first clue that you had a connection to the Levy brothers."

He cursed in Spanish. "I was stupid like Paco. But you, An-goose. You can't just leave us be." He picked up the gun and waved it at me. "You ruin everything. I kill you for that!"

"No!" Moises said, grabbing for Ricardo's gun hand. "Maybe we can make a deal."

Ricardo wouldn't let him get hold of the gun, pushing him away. I watched them both, looking for an opportunity to tackle Ricardo. But a low glass coffee table stood in the way.

"Mi amor. What's past is past." Moises looked at me. "What can you offer us?"

"He offer us shit," Ricardo said. The gun was clenched in his hand, but at least it wasn't pointing at me. "Is only one way out. We trade Mr. FBI for our freedom. We leave here with diamonds, and FBI forget us."

Trading me was better than shooting me, but the FBI wouldn't deal. "Can't do that," I said.

"I spoke to Baruch," Moises said. "He and Jacobo will drop the charges if they get the diamonds back. Without a theft, there's no crime." He turned to me, a pleading look on his face. "Right Angus?"

Before I could answer, Ricardo jumped in. "You can no' trust your brothers, Moises," he said. "Not after how they treat you all these years. They try to keep us apart, make you marry, watch you always."

I saw Moises hesitate, and I stepped in. "I have a brother myself," I said. "He's five years younger than I am. Kind of a screwup. But I'd do anything for him. I think you can count on your brothers, Moises. I've talked to them."

"Only as long as I have the diamonds. That is all they care about. They won't accept me. They never have."

"Don't be too sure of that. Baruch's already come around. He knows about you and Ricardo, and he feels bad about how you got forced into doing things. And Jacobo? Well, if he gets his diamonds back, I think that'll improve his mood considerably."

"If we give back diamonds, we have nothing," Ricardo said. "And we go to jail."

"If you don't come in on your own, you certainly will." I held up my hand. "I can't negotiate, you understand. But we can talk things through, see where we stand."

I waited, and neither of them argued. So I turned to

Moises. "Have you done anything that a judge would consider criminal other than steal the diamonds from your brothers?"

"I am with Ricardo. Anything he has done, was for me. And me for him."

"That's a nice attitude. But let's stick with the facts, for now. Were you the one who poisoned Jacobo's lunch?"

"My cousin, she get a girl to work the cart," Ricardo said, jumping in. He rested the gun on his lap. "I show her which one is Jacobo, because he is worst brother. I wish he die from tuna!"

"*Cierra la boca*, Ricardo," Moises said. "Jacobo is still my brother, no matter what." He looked at me. "I knew he was going to be made sick, but I didn't know how."

"*Es verdad*," Ricardo said, putting his hand on Moises's arm. "I am only criminal here." He rubbed the corner of his eye with a knuckle, then handed the gun to Moises. "If I go with you, Moises goes free?"

"Mi amor," Moises began, but Ricardo waved a hand at him.

"Let An-goose talk," Ricardo said.

Moises placed the handgun on the low table and pushed it toward me. I leaned forward and retrieved it, and for the first time that night I thought we might be moving toward a safe ending.

I looked back at Ricardo. "How closely did you work with your cousin?" I asked him.

He crossed his arms over his chest. "She don't trust me much. She still think I am little boy who play with dolls." He sneered. "She don't know I am tough, that I am listening all the time. I am careful, I don't do hardly nothing that is against the law, but I know what she does."

"Then you talk to the District Attorney, see what kind of deal you can make. I can't make this sweet for you, Ricardo. You're an accessory to murder; you're trafficking in drugs; you were involved in this diamond theft. But if you didn't kill Paco, and you have some information on your cousin and Nilady Cruz that you can trade, then maybe, at some point, the two of you could be together, you could go back to Mexico."

"I don't want to go back there," Moises said. "There is nothing back there for me."

"Sure there is," I said. "You have a son. Two brothers. Nephews and a niece. But who knows? Maybe you can both stay here. Get a job in a jewelry store or something."

"He designs," Ricardo said proudly. He held up the bracelet. "He make this."

"There you go," I said to Moises. "You have a lot of contacts in the jewelry business. While Ricardo gets his legal affairs sorted out, you find someone who will sponsor you for a visa based on your artistic talent. Then when this is all resolved, you can both move up to that house in Pennsylvania, if that's what you want."

I looked from Moises to Ricardo and back. "Well?"

They put their heads together and began speaking in low, rapid Spanish. I hoped that Zolin was able to get what they were saying because I couldn't catch a bit of it. I looked down at the handgun in my lap. It was a Hi-Point 9 mm with a polymer frame, and I slipped the magazine out and checked it. All eight bullets were in place.

I glanced at the Mexicans. They were both still deep in conversation. I locked the magazine back in place and wrapped my hand around the grip, my finger close to the trigger.

Their conversation became more heated, all in Spanish. Then, without warning, Moises slapped Ricardo across the cheek.

I expected Ricardo to go ballistic—jump up, start screaming, punch his boyfriend. But instead, he stared at Moises for a long beat, then burst into tears.

Moises wrapped his arms around Ricardo, and Ricardo rested his head on Moises's shoulder. "We will go," Moises said to me. "The diamonds, they are in a briefcase in the bedroom upstairs."

"I'll take care of that once I hand you guys over." I stood up, and without thinking I went to holster the Hi-Point, then remembered all I was wearing was a pair of boxer briefs.

I motioned them around so that I was between them and the dining room table. I laid the handgun on the table so I could have my hands free. "I have to pat you down now," I said.

Ricardo raised his hands above his head, and Moises did the same. When I was satisfied that neither had a weapon, I picked up the Hi-Point again and motioned them toward the door. "Let's step out into the courtyard," I said, hoping that Zolin was passing the word on to the other agents.

Moises opened the front door, and over his shoulder I saw Roly, Ferdy, and Vito there, weapons drawn. Roly stepped up with a pair of handcuffs. "Moises Levy, you are under arrest," he said, slapping his cuffs on the Mexican's wrists. Ferdy followed suit with Ricardo.

Roly read them both their rights as he led them down the driveway and into the Bureau SUV. When they were gone, Vito looked through the door from the courtyard at me. I must have looked pretty ridiculous there, barefoot and naked but for my tight-fitting briefs, still holding Ricardo's Hi-Point.

"You just can't keep your clothes on, can you, rookie?" Vito asked, shaking his head. "Get dressed. We've still got a lot of work to do here."

32

TINY DIAMONDS

I retrieved my clothes and my gun from the courtyard and carried them into the downstairs bathroom in Parfitt's townhouse. I put everything back on except the bulletproof vest, then joined Wagon in the dining room.

Vito came downstairs, carrying a locked briefcase, his cell phone cradled under his neck. "We're gonna need you to verify the contents of the briefcase," Vito said, and I assumed he was talking to one of the Levy brothers. "Can you come up here and bring a list of what should be inside?"

He listened for a moment. "Yeah, I'll bet you would. Here's Agent Green; he'll give you the address." He handed the phone to me. "Baruch Levy."

"Good evening, Mr. Levy." I read him the address, and asked, "Do you need directions?"

"We have GPS in rental car," he said.

Sheryl pulled the Bureau surveillance car into Parfitt's driveway, then came inside. At least she'd dressed to blend with the beach crowd, in a casual top and shorts that showed off her tan. "You go next door with Sheryl to clean up the place," Vito said. "Make it look like we were never there."

Sheryl found a pair of blue latex gloves and started scrubbing down the kitchen while I picked up my gear from the guest bedroom and bath. Then I moved Tom's furniture back into place, vacuumed, and dusted. By the time we were done, the place was sparkling.

When we finished, Sheryl went back next door, and I called Tom and told him he could come home. I opened the garage door for him, and stood at the side of the driveway as he pulled in.

He was in pretty good spirits for a guy who'd just risked having his home blown up. Still perfectly groomed, looking like he'd just come from a dinner date at a private club. He popped the trunk, and I lifted his suitcases back out, ignoring the persistent ache in my chest.

"Before I go inside, tell me what the damage is," he said.

"No damage at all," I said.

"Really?"

"I wouldn't lie to you," I said, smiling.

He raised his eyebrows. "Perhaps not," he said. I led him back into his townhouse, and even made sure that the panel in the guest bathroom was securely in place. Then I retrieved my duffle bag and went back out to the living room.

"You never know what's going on around you," Tom said. "All those times in Lazy Dick's I saw Ricardo and his pals flirting, I never once considered there was something nefarious happening."

"You had no reason to." I stuck out my hand to shake

his. "I appreciate everything you did, Tom, and I apologize if anything I did or said mislead you."

"I won't hug you, because I can see your chest is still bothering you," Tom said, taking my hand. "But I reserve the right to take you out to dinner again sometime."

"It would be my pleasure." We shook hands, and then I carried my bag next door to see if there was anything else I could do. Wagon, Sheryl, and Zolin had left in the surveillance car, but Vito was sitting at the kitchen table with Jacobo and Baruch Levy.

Baruch was still in his neon surfer clothes, but both he and his older brother looked sad and tired. Vito handed Jacobo the briefcase, and he entered a combination. I held my breath for a second as the lid popped open, hoping we wouldn't see another empty case.

I let my breath out at the sight of dozens of small felt drawstring bags. "You won't mind if Agent Green keeps our own record of the inventory?" Vito asked, though it wasn't really a question.

"No problem," Baruch said.

Vito knew more than I did about diamonds, and he helped me as Baruch read off the notes accompanying each package—how many carats were enclosed, along with the color, clarity, and cut. He handed each stone to his brother, who examined it with a jeweler's loupe and confirmed it was correctly labeled, and also matched their own inventory.

It was almost 11:00 p.m. by the time we finished. "What will happen to our brother now?" Baruch asked. "Can he come home with us?"

I shook my head. "Not right now, at least. You'll have to check with the District Attorney's office and see if they're pressing any charges, and if so, what the bail arrangements are. I doubt he'll be able to leave the United States, though."

"He is our brother," Baruch said. "We will help him."

"And his wife and son," Jacobo said. "This will be very sad for her, to know that her husband has lied to her."

"I'm sure he'll be grateful for your help," I said.

"So, if there is no theft, there is no need to keep the diamonds as evidence, correct?" Baruch asked.

"There is still a criminal case," Vito said. "But I spoke to the Special Agent in Charge earlier, and he authorized me to release the diamonds back to you. We don't want to be responsible for them."

"Very good," Jacobo said. I walked them out to their car, and as I watched it back down the driveway and join the flow of traffic on A1A, my phone rang. Once again, Danny was calling while I was working. But this time it didn't matter, because Vito was busy relaying information to the SAC and wouldn't need me for a few minutes.

I answered as I walked into the courtyard. "Hey, Danny. Tell me what's going on." I sat down on a padded lounge chair and wiped off a thin coating of sand. The traffic on A1A was a comforting murmur, and the night air was full of the smell of salt water and auto exhaust.

"They kept me at the police station for hours," he said. "I kept telling them the same story, over and over again. My brother the FBI agent told me to watch out for the skimmer, I saw Rocket use it, then I found it."

"Where's Rocket?"

"It looks like he skipped town," Danny said. "He never showed up for work, and the cops kept grilling me about where he might have gone. But I had no idea. Finally the detective said I could go, and I went home and crashed."

He hesitated for a moment, then said, "I kept wanting to call you again, convince you to come up and rescue me."

"I wanted to come," I said. "It was killing me to know you were in trouble and I couldn't help you more."

"That's okay. Somewhere around the third or fourth hour I was at the station I realized that I couldn't keep depending on you. I'm twenty-one years old and I should be able to stand on my own two feet."

"That's good, Danny. Really good. But I'll always be your big brother."

"I know. It was funny, I started worrying more about you. That maybe I ought to come to Fort Lauderdale and look after you for a while. How are you doing?"

"I'm all right." I tried to lie back on the lounge chair without hurting my rib too much. "My case is finishing, and I feel really good about that. Still flying high from everything. And you know what? I learned that I'm a real FBI agent, bro. Like holy fuck, I can do this job."

"I never doubted you, Angus. You can do anything you set your mind to."

"I'm not the only one, Danny. So can you."

"Yeah, I think so too. I appreciate everything you've done for me, I really do. But I can't keep leaning on you. I looked over my school work and I figured out that if I knuckle down and stop screwing around, I could get it done in half the time, and I can pick up some extra shifts at La Scuola now that Rocket's gone. I'm going to work my ass off so that I can have enough money for Italy. And I want to pay you back everything you've given me."

I put my hand over my heart, even though Danny couldn't see the gesture. "Oh, my God, my baby brother is growing up!"

"I'm not swearing off girls, though," he said. "No worries about me joining your team, or becoming a monk or anything. I'm just gonna focus on work."

I laughed. "If you ever do change your mind, bro, we could make a killer team here in Fort Laud."

Danny laughed too, and it was great to hear my brother sound happy, for the first time in a while. "I'll keep that in mind, Angus. Catch you on the flip side, bro."

I hung up, but stayed in the chair for a couple of minutes. The warm, humid air was like a comfortable blanket, and I realized that my body still had a lot of healing to do. I was tempted to doze off right there, but when Roly returned in the Bureau van, I stood up, closing my eyes for a couple of seconds as pain shot through my chest.

"How are you doing, Angus?" Roly asked as he walked into the courtyard.

"I need to sleep for at least a day," I said, and yawned.

"Let's get Vito and close up things."

We walked inside, where Vito was finishing off a bottle of water from Parfitt's fridge. "My car is back at the Bureau," Vito said. "Can you give me a ride home, Roly?"

"Sure. I'll even pick you up Monday morning." He turned to me. "How about you, Angus? We can drop you back at your house on the way."

I shook my head. "I want to decompress for a while. Maybe walk on the beach. When I'm done, I can get a cab." I looked at my watch. It was almost midnight, and Lester's shift would be ending. "Or I might be able to get a ride with a friend."

We locked up Parfitt's townhouse, and I stayed in the courtyard after they drove away. I called Lester's cell.

"G-man," he said, and the sound of his voice made me feel warm inside.

"I'm done with work," I said. "Still not up to much in the way of athletics, but I'd like to see you. Any chance you could swing past here and pick me up when you finish your shift?"

A breeze pushed through, replacing the smell of auto exhaust with pure salt water, and I thought it might be nice to live over by the ocean someday, when I could afford it.

"I'd say there's a very good chance," Lester said. I gave him the address and hung up. Then I sat back on the lounge chair, looking up at the sky. Despite all the ground light around me, I could see a couple of stars out over the ocean, tiny diamonds against a background of black.

ACKNOWLEDGMENTS

I would like to express my gratitude for being able to attend the FBI Citizens Academy, and to all the agents and support personnel who provided such incredible insight into the workings of their agency.

My critique group—Miriam Auerbach, Christine Jackson, Kris Montee, and Sharon Potts—provide valuable feedback on every piece of writing I share with them, and their words are in my head as I write and revise.

Thanks for technical help to Jim Born, though I take full responsibility for all errors and improbabilities.

Additional thanks, for various reasons, to Joe Pittman and Maryam Salim. My editor, Randall Klein, provided terrific feedback and inspiration, and I also appreciate the work of all at Diversion Books who have helped in the production of this book.

And of course, Marc, who makes it all possible.

31901060115443

CPSIA information can be obtained
at www.ICGtesting.com
Printed in the USA
BVOW11s1339071016

464420BV00002B/5/P

9 781682 303016